Praise for *The Last Tsar's Dragons*

"To include dragons in the Russian Revolution seems like the kind of inspired idea that, in lesser hands, could not possibly live up to a reader's expectations; but Jane Yolen and Adam Stemple take that idea and soar with it, spinning a tale of alternate history that is both wondrous and sublime. The book is elegant, quotable, and at the end, I simply wished for more."
—James A. Owen, author of *Here, There Be Dragons*

"Master fantasist Yolen (*How To Fracture a Fairy Tale*, 2018, etc.) and her son Stemple collaborate on a novella that merges dragons with the Russian Revolution. Cycling among the points of view of the last tsar, Nicholas II, his wife, the tsarina Alexandra, the notorious Grigori Rasputin, Leon Trotsky, and an unnamed court official, the story tells the downfall of tsarist Russia and the rise of the revolution—but if you think you know the story, think again. Because in this Russia, the tsar sends out flights of black-scaled, fire-breathing dragons to harass his enemies, especially the Jews, and Leon Trotsky (known in the book by his birth name, Bronstein) has managed to secretly raise an army of his own dragons—these are red and fighting for the revolution. Despite the high stakes, the story feels quite intimate as it leads us to gaze on each player in turn: the tsarina, a foreigner to her husband's country, plagued with worry over her ill son and believing

that only Rasputin can save him; Rasputin himself, driven by his madness, lusts, and ambition; Bronstein, who struggles to keep hold of the weapon he has given to the revolution; and our nameless court dignitary, whose hatred of Rasputin drives much of the action. The dragons themselves are never afterthoughts—their effect on the characters, even when they are not present, worms its way into nearly every scene—but they are also not the players of the drama. Like the impending revolution, their presence simply hangs over the characters with the shadow of brutal, impersonal violence. Where the characters end up is not surprising—we know the history, after all—but getting there is delightful, carried along by crisp, tight prose and the authors' marvelous imaginations."
—*Kirkus*

"Vivid, gripping and actually riveting as the Red Danger takes a whole new meaning here. Loved it."
—*The Book Smugglers*

Praise for *Pay the Piper*
by Jane Yolen and Adam Stemple

"Yolen and her son, a professional musician, have produced a rollicking good riff on the Pied Piper. . . . An entertaining as well as meaty read."
—*Booklist*

"Jane Yolen, a mistress of fantasy, has teamed up with her rock-and-roll musician son to develop a series crossing classic tales with contemporary music. This debut effort is a thriller."
—*The Washington Post*

"Veteran storyteller Yolen works with her musician son on this new interpretation of the Pied Piper of Hamelin story that will intrigue those [who] enjoy retellings of familiar stories or are lured by tales of the Faerie realm."
—*VOYA*

"[A] swift and entertaining read . . . skillfully blends ancient magic with music and contemporary teen life."
—*KLIATT Magazine*

Praise for *Troll Bridge* by Jane Yolen and Adam Stemple

"Drawing elements from 'The Twelve Dancing Princesses' and 'The Three Billy Goats Gruff,' [Yolen and Stemple] give folklore a modern spin in an entertaining tale."
—*Booklist*

"Fairy tale fantasy master Yolen teams up with her son Stemple to offer an entertaining and engaging story."
—*VOYA*

THE LAST TSAR'S DRAGONS
JANE YOLEN & ADAM STEMPLE

THE
LAST TSAR'S
DRAGONS

JANE YOLEN
ADAM STEMPLE

TACHYON
SAN FRANCISCO

Cover art "Simplification Project" copyright © 2015 by Anabelle
Gerardy
Interior and cover design by Elizabeth Story

Tachyon Publications LLC
1459 18th Street #139
San Francisco, CA 94107
415.285.5615
www.tachyonpublications.com
tachyon@tachyonpublications.com

Series Editor: Jacob Weisman
Project Editors: Jill Roberts and James DeMaiolo

Print ISBN: 978-1-61696-287-6
Digital ISBN: 978-1-61696-288-3

First Edition: 2019
10 9 8 7 6 5 4 3 2 1

Printed in Canada

For Betsy, Ari, David: your kind of history—with dragons.
For Jacob Weisman & Jim DeMaiolo & Jill Roberts, in gratitude.
And Elizabeth Harding, for everything.

—JY

For Red Mark, comrade.

—AS

YOUR REVOLUTION IS A LIE.

There were no heroes, no great causes. Just slaughter, suffering, death.

And dragons.

Oh, you thought those a myth? Tales your grandfather told you?

No, the dragons were real. *Bolvan*, the dragons are why you won! The only reason there aren't dragons today is that Uncle Joe slaughtered the reds during the Great Purge, and in '23 a pack of larcenous Chinese eunuchs blew up the dragon barns in the Forbidden City while trying to destroy evidence of their embezzlement.

I see you smiling, you indoctrinated young fool. You see a man who has turned against the revolution that employed him for nearly thirty years. A man convicted of corruption and treason and worse, and you think I would say anything to avoid the firing squad. But in truth, I am old and weary and no longer afraid to die. I just want someone to know the truth.

So it falls on you, young man, to hear the true tale of the revolution, dragons and all.

THE DRAGONS were harrowing the provinces again. They did that whenever the tsar was upset with the Jews. He would go down to the dragon barns himself with an oversized golden key and unlock the stalls. He always made a big show of it.

At his grand entrance, the dragons, black and shiny as bats, with the same kind of pinched faces, stomped about, stirring the dust, 'til the royal barns felt like a sandstorm. Bits of straw, dung, and gold dust filled the air. Saturated it. As the dragons were fond of the gold dust, the tsar had ordered thousands of coins ground on a weekly basis to keep them happy.

That the gold dust—as opposed to the dung and straw—made the dragon handlers sick was never the tsar's concern. Dragon boys could be found in every corner of the kingdom. Mujecks, peasants, vied for a place at the palace. They loved serving the tsar. Indeed, there were lines of them each morning trying to get in to see him for work, though he left their hiring to the man in charge of the barns.

Dragon boys knew to walk quietly amongst the great creatures. Dragons might be big, but they were sensitive in their own dens, prone to fits of weeping globules of golden tears and spitting fire. Occasionally a dragon boy was caught trying to make off with one of the golden tears. For them it was a fortune. A vicious beating, and instant dismissal after, kept such thievery to the very minimum. Few tried it any more, ever since one boy— by all accounts quite popular—died from his beating. It hadn't been a mistake but by the tsar's insistence.

The tsar was not a quiet man. He was used to being obeyed—by men and women, children, dogs, horses. Even his wife, the German woman, did what she was told. Well, most of the time. She was German, after all.

He expected the same from the dragons. So he never bothered to learn to walk softly, speak in a hushed tone. Indeed, why should he? He was the supreme ruler of the Russians, the heir to fortunes, his name used in praise at all the Russian churches, next to God's. Sometimes even over God's. His priests cautioned about that, but the tsar didn't worry.

"God's kingdom is there," he would say, waggling his fingers towards the sky. "Mine is here." His hand indicated all of the earth.

In the dragon barn, he called out to the dragons, flinging open their stall doors dramatically, the barn doors—cumbersome and heavy—having already been opened by his servants.

"Go, my children! Go!"

The tsar liked to call the dragons his children—peasants and dragons alike. The peasants seemed to respond well to that. The dragons? Well, as they say in the Caucasus, *If your faithful friend turns into a flaming shirt—do not cast it off.* Like most peasant sayings, they are competent metaphors.

Tsar Nicholas flung his arm upward, outward, though having no sense of direction, he usually pointed toward Moscow. That would have been a disaster if the dragons had been equally dense. But of course they were not. Like birds, they were aligned to the air's own map. They were never lost. Though, as the mad monk once said: *Never lost, but perhaps bothered for a few days.* They'd been trained on Jewish flesh, so unlike the hardy Russian stock. Jewish prisoners, mostly moneylenders and rabble-rousers, jailed for their sins.

So the dragons took off, galloping out the door, filling the barn behind them with gold dust that left the dragon boys coughing madly. But the tsar—with the lack of care of all his kind—simply put a silken handkerchief over his sacred nose and mouth and headed back up the secret stairs that ran between his apartment and the barn.

He hastened to look out of the windows in his study as the dragon horde rose into the air.

So light, he always thought, *for such huge creatures. Their bones must be as hollow as birds.*

The sky darkened as the vee of dragons covered a great swath of the heavens. Bits of golden-flecked dung fell like stars behind them. The peasants would rush to pick it up and cart it back to their holdings. It was said to be potent for growing both beets and babies. Gather a bunch of it and maybe the dust could turn into enough to buy a whole new garden. Or wife.

Watching the dragons, the tsar smiled. He felt his heart beat to the rhythm of their wings. As he so often said to the tsarina—"It is as if I am there, flying aloft with them.

"When I was a boy, we believed only birds and bats flew."

She always smiled when he said that, so unlike him, because Tsar Nicholas was not known for his imagination. "And butterflies and bees," she teased.

He smiled down at her fondly. "Oh my darling Sunny," he said, watching his strong-willed wife melt at that pet name. It might have been because the words were so unexpected from someone who was known to be precise and punctual, in the extreme. But she also knew how much he valued her thoughts on important matters. She always gave him something to think about, something the generals or the councilors usually failed to consider.

He didn't tell the men that, of course. Or how much he relied on her. It was his little secret with the tsarina.

As the tsar watched the lead dragon turn the vee toward the provinces, he did not notice the peasants below gathering the dung. Not until he heard them reciting the old rhyme,

> *Fire above, fire below,*
> *Pray to hit my neighbor.*

It works, he thought, *equally well for dragons as military planes and their munitions. And it certainly rhymes splendidly in the dialect.*

He turned from the fading scene of departing dragons and looked at himself in the full-length mirror along the far wall.

Something was not quite right.

He gave a little tug to the bottom of his tunic, then smoothed it with his right hand. Precision and punctuality had been drilled into him as a child. And, as expected of all the tsars, he was also full of batiushka and grozny. Batiushka—a good little father to his people, always ready to express interest in their welfare and problems. And grozny—yet larger than life, imposing, awe-inspiring, terrible, like the God of the Old Testament.

Another tug on his jacket, as he thought: *I labor hard to be both.*

But most imagination was beyond him. It had not

been part of his upbringing. No tutor would have lasted who suggested he learn such a thing. As if imagination could be taught.

"For poets, actors, and women, I suppose," he told the mirror. "And Jews. I am the tsar. I need facts, not fairy stories. I outgrew those when I was still a young boy." Then he grinned at his image. "Maybe not Kostchai the Deathless." As he'd once said to his nanny, "A tsar should live forever." She'd snapped back, "Not all tsars deserve it." He never told his mother or father what she said, but he remembered.

It was time to get ready for his trip. He hated to leave the family, his beloved wife, the dragons. But duty called. It was what he was born to, what he would die for. He promised himself he would wear it well to the very end.

Or perhaps, I shall live forever. If I deserve it.

The tsarina glanced out of the window as the dragons rose into their long, black line. She loved to watch them, too, but for reasons very different than her husband's. *So graceful*, she thought. *Ils sont si gracieux. Like geese going south, if you ignored the dragons' long tails, the smoke that trailed behind them. If you didn't try to change their grunting sounds into the hysterics of geese.*

She was well used to ignoring aspects of things she didn't like. That was part of what a good ruler did. Hold one's nose and think of Our Lord. She had done that enough times to have earned her rightful place in Eternity.

She chuckled to herself. It was also how she had so many children. How she got through her days in court. Russian courtiers were not an easy crowd to swallow, jumped-up peasants, the lot of them. And their French—*incroyable!* She had tried to be interested in their problems, their troubles, but she'd made few friends. They spoke Russian quickly when around her, which they knew she didn't know well. She could have understood them in German or English or French. Or if written, she had a good sense of Latin and Greek. But Russian—even after so many years—was often still a puzzle to her. And usually at the worst moments. She was too shy to ask the Russians to speak more slowly. Or to ask the meaning of a word. She hated feeling incompetent. Languages had always been her best subject. She was right to be proud of her way with many tongues. But Russian. . . .

Yes, she greatly preferred the dragons with their grace and grunts to the Russian courtiers.

There were many days when she longed for home. Her childhood home. The family castle in Darmstadt remained enshrined in her memory. She knew the court called her German Alix. They showed their hatred of her at every formal occasion. Whispering as she went past, never inviting her to take tea.

But, she reminded herself, *I am Tsarina, not any of you.* Though of course Mother Dear, that witch of a mother-in-law, outranked her because of the barbaric Russian customs.

She felt herself getting cold, and then her jaw began to ache again. A headache was starting, a clear sign that she needed another bit of her powder in its glass of warm water. Bless Father Grigori who had discovered the Veronal for her. This last year it had gotten her through many difficult days.

Glancing once more out of the window, she saw the last of the black vee disappearing over the horizon. She shivered with some kind of unholy delight watching them on their way to harrow the Jews, those filthy carbuncles on Russia's behind. Even worse than those in her beloved Germany. She remembered some of the stories dear Papa used to tell about them, though none she could repeat in polite society. Not as a woman. Not as the tsarina.

But there was no need to. The stories—truths, really—were well known. Darling Nicky had even commissioned a pamphlet about it—their degradations, the murder of innocent Christian babies to use the holy blood to make their disgusting crackers. *Matza*, it was called. Silly word for such a foul deed. She crossed herself three times to get rid of the image of those poor babies, then shivered, and not from the cold. She hoped the dragons would manage to kill a lot of the Jews this time. The whole lot of them.

There was a sudden, horrible cry from the nursery two floors above.

An answering frightened scream, possibly one of the younger nurses.

The tsarina turned sharply at the sound.

Alexei must have fallen again.

With dignified speed—she'd never been a fast walker, leg injuries as a child had defined her careful gait—she headed straight off to the nursery, two floors and a long hallway away from where she was now. The doctors predicted that Alexei would not die of his diseased blood.

But what did they know? Her own brother had died of the same filthy illness. And German doctors, even the ones unable to save her brother, were much, much better than the Russians.

This time I will persuade Nicky to bring German doctors here. Once she set her mind to it, she could always make it happen. But she always chose her battles carefully.

There. One set of stairs done and no more screams.

She stopped to catch her breath.

And then she thought—as she often did—that there was no way they could let Alexei become the tsar. Even the smallest of arguments wore him down. His own baby tantrums could turn into days of distress. The stress of being tsar would certainly kill him.

She would not, could not, think about the possibility of an early death for her son.

She remembered hearing from her tutor how King Henry VIII of England's sick son died very young and how his half sisters, Mary and Elizabeth had nearly ruined the kingdom, squabbling over who would get to rule after him. Would it possibly be the same if Alexei assumed the throne? *When* he assumed the throne. Only with three living sisters to squabble, not just two? Would the Russians—barbarians—accept the idea of a woman on the throne? Even with her own grandmother the longest -reigning monarch in the civilized world?

She set off on the second set of stairs, wondering as she often did if she at this age might have another child.

It would have to be another son. She sighed aloud. It was her burden and her duty.

Without noticing, she shuddered. Touched her right temple, which was throbbing.

Best she get the girls married off—or at least promised—as soon as possible, to strong princes.

Halfway up the second set of stairs, she took a deep gulp of air and pushed for more speed from her weak legs. *This disease of Alexei's might kill us all someday.*

Now in the hall, she went along as fast as she could, hoping the bruising might not have hurt Alexei so much this time. That his knees wouldn't swell up.

The doctors had been hinting at an improvement. The aspirin powder they had been giving Alexei regularly was something new, processed in Germany, so she knew it had to be of good quality—was especially made for such pain, such swelling.

For a while it had worked. But only a little while.

But Father Grigori, blessed be that holy man, had demanded the doctors be kept away. And as God so favored him, she had gone along with his advice.

And. . . .

She'd reached the door of the nursery. It was slightly ajar. She listened for a second, heard no cries, no sobbing. Alexei seemed to be doing better under the priest's care rather than the doctors'. Less bruising, better appetite. . . .

But that cry that she'd been able to hear two floors away . . . that was not a sound she'd heard before. Perhaps the pain had maybe gotten worse. Ach! It was so difficult to know what to do.

I will put it in God's hands. That can never be wrong.

She crossed herself again in the Russian way, though even after so many years in Russia, it felt like an affront to God. But otherwise, she was happier in this old religion than the newer Lutheranism she'd been born into. If it had only been the Russian Orthodox church, her dear husband, their daughters and son, she would have been content living in this barbaric country.

But the people. . . .

Grandmama, she sighed, *I am trying to be strong like you. But underneath that breath of courage. . . . These people will be the death of me.*

She would have taken the Veronal and lain down for the rest of the morning, but she knew she could do nothing until her darling Alexei was tended to. And after that, a farewell dinner with her husband, who was to be off in the morning playing at soldiers with his popinjay generals, in wars they never quite seemed to win.

She trusted in the Lord, repeating that over and over in time to the sound of her feet on the carpet, on the steps, on the parquet floor. "I trust in the Lord. I trust in the Lord." She repeated it like an instruction booklet. It was the only way she could be certain that His will would be done.

Of course the Jews are all safe, having seeded their shtetls with drachometers—*early warning devices that only they could have cobbled together,* I thought as I washed my hands in the basin. I checked the mirror casually. "You goat," I said to myself sternly. "Think this through." I was always stern with myself on the tsar's business. *Rather, the devices were put together by cannibalizing a German invention.* "That's more like it," I said. "Trust the Jews to steal an idea."

"The tsar will take that bit of Jew bait in better. Especially with his German wife." I smiled. "And yes, I know I am speaking to myself. It's the only way of holding an intelligent conversation in the palace. After all, no one else can keep up with my ideas." *Especially not the tsar.* I do not say this last out loud. *Alas, the Romanovs bred for stupidity. Rather like the British royals.*

Even though I know myself to be alone, even though I am certain I did not say anything important that could be overheard, I glanced around, suddenly afraid someone might have sneaked in. Because I know, everyone knows, that there are spies everywhere. Even my dear wife reports what I say, do, to the authorities.

After all—everyone spies. My wife spies on me. As I on her.

Riffling through the desk drawers where I kept the more secret documents, I mumbled: "I have the information about that device somewhere."

Of course that was often the problem—not getting the information, but finding the information when I needed it.

Ninotchka insists a messy desk is the sign of a disordered mind, and she constantly has the maid tidy things.

"Tidying things!" I nearly spat the words out. "That is a euphemism for hiding things where I can't find them. Just because she thinks it's messy does not mean I cannot find what I need. And right now. . . ." I glowered at the order on the desktop. "Right now," I whispered in case she might be up and about, "right now I am thinking about taking a different wife."

After a minute of sorting through the piles, I found the information I sought, under an invitation to dinner. Of course!

"Here it is: Dov Krinsky!" I remembered now. Krinsky's father had worked with a German scientist, as his chief dogsbody on experiments on something called a telemobiloscope. "A real Dusseldorf dummy!" That came out almost as a snort. The rest came tumbling after. "Yes! Yes!"

My right forefinger tapped the papers as I remembered, an old habit from a few years back when I was more spy than bureaucrat. "Hülsmeyer almost lost his shirt with the invention, forgetting to file the proper patents and papers. But the German navy got wind of it and its potential to spot oncoming ships and. . . ." I could feel my excitement spilling over and I addressed the desk companionably. "I see you are ahead of me!"

"We got this from his mother," I told the desk. "A disgusting crone of a woman. But susceptible—as they all are—to a rather large bribe."

If the desk found this display of spleen unworthy, it kept its own counsel.

"Young Krinsky himself almost got away, through the underground, on his way to the Americas with the complete set of plans, and a prototype. Leaving his family behind. Isn't that just like them?"

I held the paper up to the light, though I didn't need to actually read it. Just the first line. The rest I had memorized, just needed that bit at the beginning to remind myself.

"Krinsky's old mother died in questioning. That was done by a clumsy oaf of an examiner. Never, never let someone die if there are still questions to be answered. But not before telling us her son had died when the boat sank, along with the plans and the lessons."

I was the only one who noticed there was a strange defiance in her eyes. So I ordered a complete search of the house and found a second set of plans. I told no one else, and the men with me who might have seen something all got shipped off to the front, following the tsar's latest wrong call for soldiers. So now there were dead ends everywhere.

I didn't say any of this out loud, so the desk had no chance to laugh at this little joke. I made a face at it.

"So you don't find that amusing, Desk?" This was of course not fair to the desk, which could not read my thoughts. "You are not alone. No one else thinks I am a funny man, but the jokes are always on them."

I walked back to the mirror, straightened my coat. Shook my finger at my reflection, all the while saying to myself: *The tsar should have listened to you when you told him to gather the Jewish scientists all in one place and force them to work for Russia. Away from their families, their friends. Use them and rid ourselves of the rest.*

I saw there was lint on my jacket and tried to pick it off.

The mirror image did not look pleased and made a sour moue with his mouth. I added, "So, once again I was not heeded." Then I shouted for my man, Nikita, to deal with the lint.

"NIKITA!"

The room rang heavily with the sound, but there was no answer from him or from anyone else. *Damn! Does no one work here but me?*

And Nikita—never around when I need him.

"Servants are a pestilence," I said aloud, not caring if any of them heard.

Then I took a brush from the top drawer in the small dresser beneath the mirror and removed the lint myself, as if I were a peasant. Then I proceeded to brush down the front of my jacket with more vigor than necessary.

Checking myself in the mirror again, I laughed, "Almost presentable, if still a functionary." The mirror chuckled as well. Almost as if we were twins actually conversing.

Leaning forward, I gazed into the mirror's eyes so we looked as if we were trading secrets. I whispered, "I may have to finalize that trip I was planning to take to Germany with my wife. A second honeymoon, we will call it. A visit to the baths. An attempt at baby-making. But whatever we call it, a necessary step." I nodded and my image nodded back, indicating it was indeed a good plan.

What I didn't say was that I was afraid the tsar's star, like his mind, was dimming. And his son would not long outlast him, poor child. I had no idea who might be jumped up to tsar. Some minor prince, I supposed. But which one, and when. . . .

I must keep a careful ear out. They will always need someone like me to make the government run smoothly.

I walked toward the door, looked back over my shoulder, nodded at the full image of myself. And of course he nodded back. "*D'accord,*" I mouthed as he did.

But the word "functionary" rose up in my throat like the sick aftermath of a rancid dinner. *It is dust in their royal mouths. But without us, there is no government, as many an autocrat has found out to his dismay.*

My mirror twin smiled. It was not a pleasant smile. More snake than courtier.

We silently oil the wheels of their progress. And they reward us to do it. But not enough. Never enough.

Hmmm, I think I will try my hand at poetry. The royals profess to love it. On the other hand, by the looks of some of the toughs proclaiming their allegiance to the rebels, I wonder if they would know what to do with a poem other than use it to wipe their bums.

At the desk again, I picked up the papers about Krinsky and shook them as if interrogating the sentences.

If I cannot save my position, this early batch of Krinsky's notes on the telemobiloscope and drachometer could be my passport to a richer life. Our passport. Ninotchka's and mine. I understand the Germans can be very liberal with their rewards for scientific invention.

I headed out the door and into the hall, going once more to see the tsar.

Or as I ofttimes call him in the echo chamber of my heart, His Royal Graciousness High Buttinsky, but carefully, of course, and never aloud. I know that I am not irreplaceable.

But all the while, I silently reminded myself: *When one works for the tsar, one must always restate the obvious.*

He has no imagination and a limited grasp of facts. And I know that once in the Presence Room, I'll certainly have to wait at least an hour to be announced, as the news of the dragons' success or failure will already have been brought by courier.

This time it took an hour and fifteen minutes by my pocket watch before I was signaled in to speak with the tsar.

By then he was in a foul mood. He had consulted with the generals, and the news he had of the dragons was not good. Deprived of their natural Jewish prey, the black horde had taken once more to raking the provinces with fire.

This time, or so it was announced by one of the generals who spoke to the very small smattering of officials, it had cost the country a really fine opera house, built in the last century and fully gilded, plus a splendid spa with indoor plumbing, two lanes of Caterina-the-Great houses, plus the servants therein. And the roads—as if they had not been already bad enough.

But as the general added, "Thank the good Lord it is winter," as if this changed everything about the disaster.

All about me the old men, the top princes and administrators, nodded their heads sagely, several even crossing themselves as if this alone would ward off disastrous news.

❖

Only later in my own rooms once more did I understand what he meant was "Thank the good Lord it is winter— all the hoi and most of the polloi are at their homes here in the city and not in their summer dachas where they would have been easy pickings. No, rather they are safe and sound in the city. They will not join any revolt."

We all knew that the smoke in the provinces—like a bad odor—would hang over those towns for a week or more. A daily, deadly reminder of the folly of dragons. When the people who owned summer houses in the province went to check out their houses, they could not possibly be pleased. And who would they blame? Was I the only one who worried about it? In whispers and insinuations, their wrath would most certainly land on His Royal High Carelessness.

Of course, I pointed out some of this to the tsar at the time, but carefully, as I wanted my head to remain firm on my shoulders. At least until my new wife wore me out.

Bowing lower than protocol demanded, I said, "Do you remember, Gracious One, what I said concerning the Jewish scientists?"

The tsar stroked his beard and shook his head. Then,

instead of giving me an answer, he mumbled a few words to the mad magician, Rasputin.

I held Father Grigori's name unspoken in my mouth, then spit it out. It was not so much a greeting as invective. But that monk, that priest of magics, said nothing in return, his own position secure because he was a favorite of the tsarina and her only son, the tsarevitch, the child with the bleeding sickness.

I waited to see if the tsar would turn to ask to hear my information again. If he would only remember the conversation we had a week ago. I could feel the pages of Krinsky's invention crackling in my jacket, eager to speak out.

I waited some more, this time eyes closed, in anticipation, in hope. But when I opened them again, it was to see the tsar and his closest advisors—several generals and Rasputin—abruptly leaving. To plan his next war, I supposed. On the Jews? On the Continent? Or on the rebels who like fleas were multiplying as we stood in uncertainty here?

Then I knew for certain: *Our little father has become an absent parent. With his catastrophic leadership, his choice of a German wife, his lack of a hardy heir, his waxing and waning attention. This war will no doubt have as little effect as the last.*

"But Tsar Nicholas II is always trying." I realized with a start that I'd said that aloud. But as no one was still standing near, it put me in no danger.

And then I thought privately: *The tsar is very trying.* I smiled, but kept it very small and contained. One must never laugh openly at the tsar. Even in private it can be dangerous.

I began the long walk back to the Presence Room door, thinking: *Of course, I have no ability to effect changes straight on, not like the ruler of a country. I must wait and wheedle to get what I want. But even with all his power, look what the tsar accomplishes. Nothing. He sends troops of loyal Cossacks to harry the Jews on the ground. He sends a murder of dragons by air. Nyet, nothing. So he does it again for more nothing.*

Stepping into the now-empty hallway, my thoughts came faster and faster: *A man who keeps doing the same thing and expecting different results must be mad. Or at least not overly endowed with brains.*

And the honest second thought I had—which quite surprised me—was that I was certain that Rasputin thought the same thing. He was not a man silent about his opinions. But he was a man who could use the church and magic to keep him safe.

I only have my wits.

But then I smiled. Rasputin and I have something else in common. We know that the tsar's faults do not stop either of us from cashing his chits, living comfortably at court, finding new young wives at every opportunity. I gave my own version of the monk's wolfish grin: our own wives or other men's.

Suddenly, my legs gave way and I managed to sit on one of the chairs in the long corridor placed there for the older courtiers for just such an occasion. I sat for a moment, regaining my equanimity. Working for a ruler can be difficult. Some days it is as if I am slogging through the mud. My own personal battlefield, I once confided to Ninotchka—early in our courtship. But, like the Jews in their burrows, I may become dirtied, but I am safe from the fire. So why this sudden weakness?

And then, as if that light suddenly shone through my own window, I understood what was truly afflicting me: it was an unsuspected fear. *The powerful are like dragons. Friend or foe, if their gaze is fixed upon you, you are likely to get burned.*

I would not sit here where any passerby could see my weaknesses and calculate how to destroy me. Where any gossip could begin that would be my end. I had not climbed this far up to become prey. I reminded myself of my intellect, my ability for camouflage, my strength. And when I put my hand over my breast pocket, the crackle of paper reminded me that I still had major cards in my hands.

I stood, shoulders back, head up, and went straight to my apartment. Even if I could not put any spring in my steps, I could more than manage to look like a man about important business, a man of determination and strength. Which I was. Which I am.

And at least—I reminded myself—I did not have a long way to go.

Some twelve feet below the frozen Russian surface, two men sat smoking their cigarettes and drinking peach schnapps next to a blue-and-white tiled stove. The tiles had once been the best to be had from a store—now long gone—in the Crimea, but in the half-lit burrow, the men did not care about the chips and chinks and runnels on them. Nor would they have cared if the stove were still residing upstairs in the house's summer kitchen. They were more concerned with other things now, like dragons, like peach schnapps, like the state of the country.

One man, Borutsch, was tall, gangly, and humped over because of frequent stays in the burrow, not just to escape the dragons, either. He had a long beard, gray as a shovelhead. With the amount of talking he tended to do, he always looked as if he were digging up an entire nation. Which, of course, he was.

The other, Bronstein, was short, compact, even compressed, with a carefully cultivated beard and sad eyes behind rimless eyeglasses.

Borutsch threw another piece of wood into the stove's maw, his long arms able to reach both the small woodpile and the stove without standing. Which he couldn't fully do in the burrow anyway. The heat from the blue tiles grew increasingly hotter, but there was no smoke due to the venting system that piped the smoke straight up through ten feet of hard-packed dirt. Then, two feet before the surface, a triple-branching system neatly divided the smoke so that when it came into contact with the cold air, it was no more than a wisp. Warm enough for wolves to seek the three streams out, but as they scattered when there were dragons or Cossacks attacking the villages, the smoke never actually gave away the positions of the burrows.

"You ever notice," Bronstein, began, "that every time we ask the tsar to stop a war—"

"He kills us," Borutsch finished for him, his beard jumping. "Lots of us." Bronstein nodded in agreement and was about to go on, but Borutsch didn't even pause for breath. "When he went after Japan we told him, 'It's a tiny island with nothing worth having. Let the little *mazzikim* who think they're descended from the sun god keep it. Russia is big enough. Why try to add eighteen square miles of nothing but volcanoes and rice?'"

Bronstein took off the oval eyeglasses that matched his pinched face so well and idly smeared the dust from one side of the lenses to the other with an old handkerchief. "Well, what I mean to say is—"

"And this latest. His high mucky-muck Franz falls over dead drunk in Sarajevo and never wakes up again, and all of a sudden Germany is a rabid dog biting everyone within reach." Borutsch gnashed his teeth at several imaginary targets, setting his long beard flopping so wildly that he was in danger of sticking it in his own eye. "But why should we care? Let Germany have France. France let that midget monster loose on us a century ago; they can get a taste of their own *borscht* now."

"Yes, well—"

But Borutsch was not to be stopped. "How big a country does one man need? What is he going to do with it? His dragons have torched more than half of it, and his 'Fists,' those damned Cossacks—" He spit the words out, then actually spit, sending sputum to sizzle on the hot tiles. "The Fists have stripped the other half clean of anything of value. While we Jews are stuck in the middle again. . . ."

"Wood and grain," Bronstein managed to interject. *The only things worth more than the dragons themselves,* he thought. *Wood in the winter and grain in the spring—the two seasons Russia gets. The nine aggregate days that made up summer and fall didn't really count.*

"Yes. So he sends us to fight and die for a country we don't own and that's worth nothing anyway, and if we happen to survive he sends us off to Siberia to freeze our dumplings off. And if we complain?" Borutsch pointed his finger at Bronstein, thumb straight. "Ka-pow."

Bronstein waited to see if the older man was going to go on, but Borutsch was frowning into his schnapps now, as if it had disagreed with something just said.

"Yes, well, that's what I wanted to talk to you about, Pinchas." Borutsch looked up at his name, his eyes sorrowful and just slightly bleary from drink. Bronstein went on. "I've got an idea."

Borutsch's lips curled upward in a quiet smile, but his eyes remained sad. "You always do, Lev. You always do."

"It's more than an idea this time," Bronstein said. "I've taken action." Borutsch's face seemed caught between curiosity and apprehension, and yet Bronstein hesitated. *Maybe I shouldn't tell him. I can go on by myself for a bit longer.*

But he knew that wasn't true. For what he wanted to do, he needed allies. He needed helpers. He needed friends. And he needed to start gathering them as soon as possible.

While Bronstein argued internally, curiosity finally won out with Borutsch. "What is this idea then, Lev? Tell me what have you 'taken action' on?"

Bronstein found that tone irksome. *This is who I want to share my dream with? A disapproving old man who talks and talks and never acts—never does anything!*

But he had to admit that this thought was neither charitable nor true. He knew the work Borutsch had done with the Black Repartition party and the Emancipation of Labor party, and he'd worked at Iskra with him in England, writing Marxist news and smuggling it into Russia.

He has always been a friend to the worker and, I have to admit, a friend to me. It's not his fault that he has grown old and his defeats hang on him like stubborn leaves on a winter tree. Frowning, he came to a decision. *He may disagree with the methods I have adopted, but he can't argue that his methods haven't failed.*

"I won't tell you," he said. But before Borutsch could ask "why not?" Bronstein continued, "I will show you."

The mad monk was not so mad as people thought. Calculating, yes. Manipulative, yes. Seductive, definitely.

He stared speculatively at himself in a gilded mirror in the queen's apartments. His eyes were almost gold.

Like a dragon's, he thought.

He was wrong. The dragons' eyes were coal black. Shroud black. Except for the dragon queen. Hers were green. Ocean green, black underwater green with a lighter, almost foamy green color in the center. But then the mad monk had never actually been down to see the dragons in their stalls or talked to their stall boys.

He didn't dare.

If there was one thing that frightened Rasputin, it was dragons. There had been a prophecy about it. And as calculating a man as he was, he was also a man of powerful peasant beliefs.

> *He who fools with dragons*
> *Will himself be withered in their flames.*

It was even stronger in the original Siberian.

Not that you can find anyone who speaks that here, he thought. Not even the peasants. But he'd not heard his native tongue for years, for he had chosen to be here in the center of the empire. *Which is where I belong.* He smiled at his reflection, his long eyeeteeth lending him a wolfish look, which suited him. From a child, he'd known he was made for greater things than scraping a thin living from the Siberian tundra like his parents.

Or dying in the cold waters of the Tura like my siblings.

Or drowning on dry land from too much homemade vodka like my cousins.

He shook off the black thoughts—which came to him too often to be a coincidence. *Prophecy, perhaps. One must always listen to prophecy.* Then he made a quick kiss at his image in the mirror.

"Now there's an enchanting man," he said aloud, but in his own dialect, just in case he should be overheard and mocked. If he feared dragons, he hated mockery. And the court was very polished in its use.

Still, his own face always did much to cheer him—as well did the ladies of the court. The ladies of the court always took him out of his black moods. As did the ladies of the pantry. And the laundry. And the field.

To say the mad monk was fond of the ladies was to say that the salmon was fond of the stream. Or that the bear was fond of the salmon.

"Father Grigori," said a light, breathy child's voice from the region of his hip. "Pick me up."

The mad monk was not so mad as to refuse the order from the tsar's only son. The boy might be ill, sometimes desperately so. The skin stretched over his pitifully thin body was often covered with bruises, as if someone had beaten him. As if anyone would dare.

But one day, Rasputin knew, one day soon the boy would be tsar. The stars foretold it. And the Lord God—who spoke to Father Grigori in his dreams of fire and ice—had foretold it as well. *And who am I*, Rasputin whispered to himself, *to argue with God?* Though he'd done so since his own boyhood. Argued, wheedled, cajoled. And God had joined in the conversations with great enthusiasm, the monk's high position being a sign of how much the Lord had enjoyed their conversations.

"As you wish and for my pleasure," Rasputin said to the boy, bending down and picking up the child. He bore him carefully, knowing that if he pressed too hard, bruises the size and color of fresh beets would form and not fade for weeks.

The boy looked up at him fondly and said, "Let's go see Mama," and Father Grigori's mouth broke into a wolfish grin. The boy was still too young to recognize what it meant. The tsarina was a tasty dish to be chewed slowly and savored, as the royals did their food, not bolted like the peasants would have done. He may have begun as a peasant, but he'd learned his lessons well. Moderation in all things. Well, at least moderation in *most* things.

"Yes, let's," Rasputin told the tsar's son. "As you wish and for *my* pleasure." He settled Alexei on his back, then practically danced down the long hall with the child riding him as if he were the tsar's own steed and not the tsarina's pet monk.

Having made it back to my apartment, I felt revived and thought about lovely Ninotchka. Perhaps she would be receptive . . . even if it was afternoon.

I recalled how we had met, not a year ago at the *Bal Blanc*, Ninotchka in virginal white, her perfect shoulders bare, diamonds circling that elegant neck like a barrier. I had been between wives—I married young and often—and was so thoroughly enchanted by her, I asked her to marry me after two afternoons. Hastily, yes. It was less than a year after my wife's death, not quite a scandal, but close enough. However, I had been besotted with Ninotchka and didn't want to chance someone else claiming her fortune. Or her virtue.

If only I had taken more time. It was not that much later I discovered that the diamonds were her sister's, and her virtue, like the diamonds, a mirage. It was only much, much later that she discovered how little money I actually had.

I suppose all those discoveries could have crippled the marriage, but we both understood the contract between us was important for our standing amongst the courtiers.

To all who saw us on a daily basis, we had to appear astonishingly in love. Even the talkative servants did not know our secret despairs.

One has to learn to be a survivor here. Otherwise, the winters are even colder.

It was very quiet in the apartment. Possibly Ninotchka was napping. Or she might be entertaining. I hoped she was available and not with some of her admirers. My earlier weakness had wakened a great desire, as if I had a need to prove my powers.

My mouth had become slightly sour, the taste of too much tea, or not enough. Perhaps from thinking too much . . . about Ninotchka. The problem with taking someone so young to wife is getting one's turn with her. Nights, of course, she is always mine, but who really knew what Ninotchka was getting up to during the day? I am not bothered by indiscretions as long as they are discreet. But I did hope it was with some rich royal, otherwise her beauty would be wasted.

I had already unlocked the door to the apartment, was partway into the Great Hall. Thought about knocking on her bedroom door, about some man scrabbling out of the bed, to hide behind hastily gathered sheets, or a pillow. While lovely Ninotchka lay there smiling her perfect smile.

Suddenly realizing: *I don't want to know*, I turned abruptly on my heel, the new boots making a squealing noise on the tiled floor. The sound was not unlike the squeal a sow makes in labor. I had watched many of them at my summer farm. A farm, thankfully not on the dragons' route. Yet.

I was good at making quick decisions. *Unlike the rest of the courtiers, sycophants and toadies all. Unlike the tsar of all the Russias, who is the worst of them all. One day he blows hot, the next cold. And they blow right along with him. Soon there will be no weather at all.* Not a bad witticism. I figured I would save it for the next dinner party—though without the tsar's name attached, of course.

I closed the door behind me with a very quiet but final *snick*.

And thinking of the weather, it felt as if there were a storm in my brain. Sometimes my thoughts worked that way. And what I was suddenly thinking about were the tsar's dragons.

I decided, not quite on a whim, to go down to the stalls and visit them, those black creatures out of nightmares. I felt that the dragons were the key. Though I wasn't sure the key to what. There is a strange, dark intelligence there. Or maybe not exactly intelligence as we humans understand it, more like cunning. If only we could harness that as well as we have harnessed their loyalty—from centuries of captivity and a long leash—much like the Cossacks, actually.

I nodded to myself, liking the dragon/Cossacks analogy. It explained so much. The Cossacks are without guile and incredibly loyal. They are all about the use of physical power, brute strength—as are the dragons, though I suspect the dragons are smarter. With a bit of luck, I might figure out this harrowing business. If the tsar listened to me this next time, he might finally make me a count. Then Ninotchka would be available in the afternoons, too. It all came down to the dragons. And the making of the plan.

As I strode down the hallway, I could feel a great grin wreathing my mouth. Making decisions, even hasty ones, always lifts my spirit. I took several deep breaths, could feel my blood began to race. There was another stirring down below. Good Lord, I felt twenty years old again.

I even began to whistle, which, if any of the royals had been in the hallway, would have been a terrible breach of protocol. . . .

And then suddenly there was the mad monk with the tsarevitch on his back.

The whistle died on my lips.

At least the two were paying me no mind. The boy riding on Rasputin as if the old man were a horse.

All the child needs is a whip. I could probably find one for him.

Just as quickly, I thought: *If the monk stumbles . . . if the boy slips off his back . . . I could be a hero.*

I began moving toward them quickly, walking more on the balls of my feet, swinging my arms.

Rasputin is the only person—noble or servant—who dares carry the child without soft lambs-wool blankets wrapped about him. I knew the boy's skin was like the oldest porcelain. It could be smashed by the slightest touch.

Well before they reached me, I saluted the monk, saying conversationally, "Father Grigori!"

He nodded back, interrupting his flow of words to the boy only briefly to call out, "Kozzle!" though it wasn't my name, only sounded somewhat similar. Then he was back to telling the tsarevitch he was a strong and just young prince and would someday be a great tsar like his father. All lies, of course, but something in his big, peasant voice made you believe it. You could read all of Siberia in his speech, and though they weren't deep thinkers, the *moujiks* of the steppes weren't liars, either.

Rasputin, it was rumored, was both.

All the while I was really ready to seize the child if necessary, thinking: *Rasputin may be just a* moujik *by birth, and he may really be as mad as they say, but I would be madder still to neglect the obeisance he demands. He has the ear of the tsarevitch. And the tsarevitch's mother, Alexandra. Perhaps more than just her ear, if you believe the rumors.*

But my mind shuddered at going that far. Besides, the tsarina was much too fastidious for any such thing. She was, after all, the granddaughter of the Upright Queen, as Victoria of England was known hereabouts. *Probably stiff as a board in bed.* But then that was said of all the English.

Though I suspect Victoria was upright only because her stays were too tight and because who would want to fumble in the dark with her? It's a wonder that randy German prince could get that many children on her. It was another small joke I would never dare say aloud, even to my few intimate friends. Because that kind of loose talk—even if meant as a joke—gets out and ruins careers, even if it is humorous. The tsar is besotted with his wife and will hear nothing bad about her, even in jest. In fact, no jests about her beloved grandmother, either. I wonder if the tsar has any sense of humor at all. Possibly it was removed at birth, like the Jews removed the foreskins of their sons.

As Rasputin came nearer, he gave me a sullen glance. Peasant to the base, but—I had to give this much to him—possessed of a kind of sardonic wit.

Still, the memory of my almost-name so recently in his mouth seemed to turn everything to ashes. As if the monk had cursed me. And me with no ability to curse him back.

Suddenly my head was filled with too many passing thoughts, all jumbled together: *The man is a monster, a peasant, and a lecher. He never addresses me by my title, but this time he looks at me with that slow, sensual grimace that drives all the women of the court wild. I wonder if it's true that he touches the louche men of the court as well with that throb of a smile. To me it looks like a serpent's smile. I trust it not at all. It has no warmth, no fellowship in it, only menace.*

As he drew even to me in the hall, he finally left off his tale-telling to the boy and whispered sharply to me, "Commend me to your young wife, she of the swan neck and the drawer full of fake pearls."

Yes, I admit I was startled at what he said.

And then, to compound the insult, the young tsar on his back tittered, as if he understood what had been implied.

At first, I thought that the monk had brought the boy inside while he did his dirty business. But I forced myself to coolly dissect what Rasputin had said. The boy would surely have reported back any such thing as an entry into someone's apartment to his mother or nannies. At his age, he would know little about the backstairs of life, though I highly suspected his sisters did.

But because of how Rasputin had phrased his taunt, I now knew what I'd only feared before. Even my own naïf Ninotchka may have fallen under Rasputin's spell. If she'd been dallying with a princeling, all could have been forgiven. But not with this Siberian monstrosity. If it was true—if it was believed by the court to be true, I would have to kill him. My legs got shaky again, but there was nowhere to sit that was close enough. I willed them to stop wobbling. Willed my mind to slow down.

My heart roiled with bitterness as I realized that soon

I would be the laughingstock of the court. If indeed I was not already. Maybe this was why the tsar hadn't listened to me. It could explain everything.

My dear Maman had said, often enough, "Don't blame the hen when the rooster crows. The fault lies with the sun." I am not certain I understood that little saw 'til this very moment. Not really.

But Maman, who could grow old sayings in the dirt outside our house, had never had any words for what I was feeling now: this cold anger thrusting its bitter hands into my heart. *For honor's sake, whether he'd had her or not, I would have to kill Rasputin. Alone or with the help of others. For Ninotchka's sake as well as my own. If word of this got around the court, I would lose my standing altogether, unless I divorced her.*

Like Jael in the Old Testament, who killed Sisera with a tent peg, I was left with no other recourse.

But how?

I felt the answer was down in the stalls with the dragons. A small shudder ran between my shoulders, but I nodded to the tsar's son atop his peasant horse. Then, deciding not to give the monk any more of my time, I turned my back—which had only moments earlier been shuddering with fear—and delivered the *cut direct*, as they liked to say in English novels, and downstairs I went.

What I hadn't known then—because I'd never been down in the dragon barns before—was that one could smell the dragons long before one saw them. It is a ripe musk, which fills the nostrils and overflows into the mouth, tasting like old boots. But it's not without its seductions. It has the smell of power. A smell that I could get used to.

The door squealed when I pulled it open, and the dragons set up a yowling to match, expecting to be fed. It was a sound somewhere between a dog whistle and a balalaika.

They were not at all what I'd expected, being black and sleek, like eels. Or maybe bats. Their long faces, framed with ropey hair, that made them seem as if they were about to speak in some Nubian's tongue. I could almost imagine Araby issuing forth instead of curls of smoke.

I remembered hearing that dragons are always hungry. That it had to do with the hot breath and needing fuel and sustaining their fires.

Grabbing a handful of what appeared to be cow brains out of a nearby bucket—a disgusting mess dripping blood and a kind of acidic potion that made one's fingers tingle—I flung the gruesome meal into the closest stall just to see what would happen.

Three or four dragons seemed to be sharing a stall, possibly because it calmed them down. And then, with a quick rustling of their giant bat wings, they swooped onto my offering. It wasn't a pretty sight. They were *hardly* dainty eaters. And they clearly did not share. The smallest dragon had little of the meat, which likely meant his chances of becoming a bigger dragon lessened at each meal.

It could be that the dragons were not *as bright as the Cossacks*, and I might have to revise my previous notions about them. I'd seen the same behavior in wolves and dogs. Politicians, too. Possibly the peasants' problem, as well.

But the rebels? Would they share equally? There was the question. If I were the rebel chief, I'd promise equality but might not be able to—or want to—deliver it once a revolution was successful.

The dragons in the stall looked up, expecting more.

And that *is the problem for any leader. Everyone is always expecting more. Especially the people at the top. The big eaters.*

I thought briefly of going back for a second handful of cow brains, but my fingers still stung badly and had a redness and an odd shine on them that made me wince just from glancing at them. I hoped I hadn't damaged the nails for good. Finding a towel hanging on a nearby peg and, assuming it was to be used, I dried off my hands, though I was certain the smell of both towel and hands was a stench that would never leave me.

Some of the solution had also dripped on my vest, burning holes across the watch pocket. I knew I was going to need to have a thorough wash and change of clothes before going to see Ninotchka, or she would never let me touch her this night.

Before I turned to go, I took a moment to gaze into the eyes of the largest one I'd fed, careful not to look down or away, nor to show fear. Fear—or so I've heard—only excited them. Like lions and tigers. Prey shows fear.

And I am no prey.

Never prey!

I stood taller, throwing my shoulders back, taking in a deep breath, and all but clicking my boot heels together like a damned Hessian, just so I wouldn't show the dragons my fear. But perhaps they smelled it on me.

I felt compelled to turn to look long in the eyes of the largest one. Perhaps I thought to tame it that way; the Lord only knows why I did it.

Its eyes were dark, like the Caspian Sea in winter, and I began to feel as if I were swimming in them. And then drowning in them. Down and down I went, eyes wide open, mouth filled with ashy water.

I knew in the sensible part of my brain that I was still standing by the dragon's stall, feet on the coarse earthen floor. Then why was my throat filling with water? Why was. . . .

I shook my head, forced myself to look away, and suddenly, as if in a sending from the Good Lord, I could see the future breaststroking towards me: hot fires, buildings in flames. The Russias burning. St. Petersburg and Moscow buried in ash. The gold leaf of the turrets on Anichkov Palace and Ouspensky Cathedral peeling away in the heat.

It was too real not to be true. It was. . . .

"Enough!" I cried aloud, not caring if anyone other than the beasts were there to hear me. "I am no mad monk baying at the moon or seeing prophesies in tea leaves or the future at the bottom of a glass of vodka. I am an educated man."

At that, I almost physically hauled myself away, finding the surface, breaking the spell. For spell it had to be.

I addressed the dragon. "I will not be guiled by your animal magic. You do not know the name of this palace nor the name of your master, the tsar. You do not even know the word for your captivity. It is only my own fears you waken in me."

The dragon turned away, not a *cut direct* but a *cut oblique*, and nuzzled the last of the cow brains at its scaly feet.

I grimaced, shook my head. I'd been wrong. There'd be no help from these creatures. And I'd be no help to them, either.

Underground, the drachometer signaled the all-clear with a sound like cicadas sighing. Bronstein and Borutsch crawled out of the burrows and into a morning still thick with dragon smoke. The two squinted and coughed and nodded to the other folks who were emerging, besmirched and bleary, from their own warrens.

No one exchanged smiles. Yes, they were alive and unharmed, but many houses had been burned in the incursion, businesses ruined, fields scorched through the snow. A stand of fine old white birch trees after which the town was named was now only charred and blackened stumps. And perhaps the next time the drachometers would fail and there would be no warning. It was always a possibility.

Drek happens, as the rabbis liked to say.

The men all grumbled and swore. Though it was not as if this pogrom against the Jews was unprecedented. Even before the dragons, there had been the tsar's Cossacks. What they didn't burn, they pillaged. At least the dragons didn't rape the women and girls. Though if the tsar ordered it done, they were certain the dragons would find a way to make that happen, too.

"May Tsar Nicholas's own house be burned down!" whispered one man before he was shushed by the others. It was said, and not without reason, that the tsar had ears everywhere.

The *babushkas* were not so full of bile. Their sighs could fill a scroll for the ark, Bronstein thought, though they were the true realists of the town. They reminded everyone of how awful the old times were before the drachometers, when tsars with names like "Great" and "Fearsome" savaged the lands with their armies. The dragons were only the latest of the tsars' weapons. When they'd appeared on the landscape, as if by magic—for how else would dragons appear?—the Jews had been nearly wiped out.

An old woman, still dusting off her black dress, raised a crooked finger and said, "May the Lord bless and keep the drachometers running," which brought them all back to reality. The invention of the drachometer, just fifteen years earlier and a primitive device by today's standards, had once again saved them.

As Borutsch's old grandmother often said, "We live in the better times."

"Better than what?" he would tease.

Then the other old women joined in with a chorus of prayers and stories, the usual Jewish response to terror. Mrs. Morowitz told the Ukranian story of Dunay, who, in a fit against the wife he adored, killed her because she was a better bow shooter than he. And then killed himself in a greater fit of despair. "And where his dear wife fell," said Mrs. Morowitz, "the River Nastsaya sprang forth. And where the hero Dunay fell, the River Danube."

Not to be outdone, old Mrs. Kahn, long a widow, told the story of a different sort of hero—Samson from the Torah. Though it ended as badly as Dunay's tale.

Hearing the old women's stories, the children gazed around, shuddering at the wanton destruction, debating whether it was better for a hero to die by his own hand in remorse or to bring down an entire temple on the heads of his enemies as he killed himself, while their older brothers and sisters made proclamations of what they would or wouldn't have done had they been faced with sudden, fiery death from above.

But not Bronstein. He'd always listened intently to the stories. They were full of truths you had to tease out from the rhetoric. He tried to imagine what it had been like in the far-off days when there was no time to get safely underground and you had to face the dragons in the open, flame, tooth, and claw against man's feeble flesh. Because he realized something the young men seemed not to: technologies fail or other technologies supplant them, and the contraption you count on one day can be useless the next.

In this the rabbis are right, he thought. *Drek really does happen.* There was only one thing you could really count on, and it certainly wasn't a cow-sized gadget that ran on magnetism and magic and honked like a bull elk in rut when a dragon came within twenty leagues.

You can only count on power. He found himself nodding at his own sudden revelation.

Those who have power stand on the backs of those who don't, and no amount of invention or intelligence could raise a person from one to the other. And where was that thought going?

He gave it a little mental push and then he had it: *to get power, you had to grab it by force. And to hold it, you had to use even more force.*

We Jews, Bronstein thought, as he led Borustch out of town, *are unaccustomed to force.* Then frowning, *Except for that which is used against us. It's why so many have already run away—to Europe, to America. They know they can't stand against the tsar and his mighty forces.* And then carefully, he whispered to himself so no one else could hear, "But what if we can? The tsar, for all his might, is only a man. And tsars and kings and strong men have fallen before. What if we Jews choose to be David against Goliath?" That made him chuckle, since he didn't believe in the Bible—its history or its religion.

"What are you chuckling about?" Borustch asked.

"The Bible," Bornstein answered, knowing it would shut his friend up. "No more talk. You will need your breath to follow me. It's a long hike."

Borutsch did not say anything more, not even to ask why he was supposed to follow or where they were going. He knew Bronstein too well for that.

Bronstein mused, *He thinks I am a dreamer like him, not a doer. But he will follow, and he will see.*

Borutsch followed.

As they climbed the hills above the shtetl, both men began to breathe heavily, their breath frosting like dragon smoke in the chill December air. Borutsch shed his outer coat. Bronstein loosened his collar. They walked on.

Entering the forest at midday, they moved easily through the massive cedars and spruce, grown so tall as to choke out the undergrowth and even keep the snow from falling beneath them.

Bronstein led confidently, though there was no actual trail. Any of his earlier footprints would have been erased by the latest snow. Also, each time he came here, he took a different route. But even that didn't matter. He would never be lost. He was as attuned to what he sought as a drachometer is to the wing beats of a dragon.

He'd never spoken aloud to anyone in this country about what he was doing. Nor written it down. Taking Borustch along this time was a first and possibly dangerous next step. But he needed a next step, and he had a plan.

If someone with the tsar's ear discovers my machinations before I am ready. . . .

The results were too dire to consider.

Signaling a halt in a small clearing, he pointed to a

fallen log. "Sit," he said, then pulled a loaf of bread from his coat pocket and handed it to Borutsch. "Eat," he said to the older man. "I go to see we aren't followed."

"If I'd known the journey was so long, I would have brought more schnapps."

Bronstein smiled and reached into his other coat pocket, revealing a flask. "I'll take it with me to ensure you'll wait."

"Be safe, then," Borutsch mumbled through a mouthful of bread.

Bronstein was not only safe but quick as well, merely trotting back to the forest's edge and peering down the slope. He could see the shtetl, still swathed in smoke, and beyond it, the thin strips of burning grain fields. There was no one working the fields at this time of year, though little enough was gotten from the harvest even when the workers labored there. The tsar's *kruks*—the "fists" Borutsch had mentioned—took the lion's share. He nodded to himself. *And the lamb's as well!* Leaving them with barely enough to starve on.

To be fair, Bronstein knew it was the same with the peasants, only the tsar did not set his dragons on them. He had a fondness for peasants. Not for Jews.

It might come to bite him in the tuchus *some day*, Bronstein thought. Then he said out loud, "May that day come soon." And he spit on the ground.

Seeing nobody climbing the slope after them, Bronstein turned back to the forest.

From field to forest. Grain to wood.

"Up," he said as he reentered the clearing and tossed the flask to Borutsch. "We are almost there."

Bronstein moved quickly now, and Borutsch struggled a bit to keep up. But as Bronstein had said, they were almost there.

They came upon a brook running swift and shallow through snowy banks. Bronstein turned downstream and paralleled it, stopping finally at an old pine tree that had been split by lightning long ago. He paced off thirty steps south, away from the stream, then turned sharply and took another thirty. Flinging himself to the ground, he began pawing through a pile of old leaves and pine needles.

"Grain and wood, Borutsch," Bronstein said. "Two of the three things that give power in this land." He'd cleared away the leaves and needles now and was digging through the cold dirt. The ground should have been frozen and resisting, but it broke easily beneath his fingers. "However, to get either one, you need the third." Stopping his digging, he beckoned to Borutsch.

Borutsch shambled over and stared into the shallow hole Bronstein had dug. "Oh, Lev," he said his voice somewhere between awe and terror.

Inside the shallow depression, red-shelled and glowing softly with internal heat, lay perhaps a dozen giant eggs. Dragon's eggs.

"There's more," Bronstein said.

Borutsch tore his gaze from the eggs and looked around. Clumps of leaves and needles that had appeared part of the landscape before now looked suspiciously handmade. Borutsch didn't bother to count the clumps but guessed there were many.

"Oh, Lev," he said again. "You're going to burn the whole world."

Rasputin bore the child into his mother's apartments. The guards knew better than to block his way. They whispered to one another when he could not hear them, calling him "Devil's Spawn" and "Antichrist" and other names. But always in a whisper and always in dialect, and always when he was long gone.

He went through the door carrying the now-sleeping child, for halfway along the "pony ride" he had felt Alexei slump, and, without stopping, he'd wrestled the boy off his shoulders and wrapped him in the soft blankets without the boy waking. It was an old trick but a good one, though the boy was getting too heavy for it to last much longer.

The five ladies-in-waiting scattered before them like does before a wolfhound. Their high, giggly voices made him smile. Made him remember the Khlysty with their orgiastic whippings. What he would give for a small cat-o-nine tails right now. He gazed at the back of the youngest lady, hardly more than a girl, her long neck bent over, swanlike, white, inviting. "Tell your mistress I have brought her son, and he is well, if sleeping."

They danced to his bidding, as they always did, disappearing one at a time through the door into the tsarina's inner rooms, the door snicking quietly shut after the last of them.

It is the sound of a latch on a box of jewels. Meant to keep you out, but if you had the key. . . . He paused and let a momentary smile ghost across his face. *Alexei is the key. The only key.* His right hand, under the blanket, made a motion as if it held a key and was unlocking something.

After a moment, Alexandra came through the same door by herself, her long face softened by the sight of the child in the monk's arms. She was a handsome woman, knew how to dress, but he suspected she was cold in bed. He'd known a woman like that back in the village, found a way to warm her to life. She'd wept when he became a monk, but he guessed she now lived contentedly with a strapping young husband who was reaping the hours of Rasputin's instruction.

"You see," he told the tsarina, "the child only needs sleep and to be left alone, not poked by so many doctors. Not given all those aspirin powders. They are from the Devil. The doctors *and* the powders. Empress, you must *not* let them at him so." He felt deep in his heart that he alone could heal the child. He knew the tsarina felt the same. She told him so all the time.

He handed her the boy, and she took Alexei from him, the way a peasant woman would take up her child, with great affection and no fear. Too many upper-class women left the raising of their children to other people. The monk admired the tsarina, even loved her, but really desired her very little, no matter what others might say. He knew that her abominable shyness made her cold, though in her own way, she was totally devoted to the tsar, that handsome, stupid, lucky man. Smiling down at her, he said, "Call on me again, Matushka, Mother of the Russian People. I am always at your command." He bowed deeply, his black robe puddling at his feet, and gave her the dragon smile.

She did not notice, though her ladies, coming back in a giggling group, did. One of them, the girl with the long neck, put a hand to her face, which was turning an inviting pink. He tucked that away for later, turning to watch the tsarina as she put the sleeping boy in her bed, not letting a single one of her ladies help her.

As Rasputin backed away, he instinctively admired the tsarina's form. She was not overly slim like her daughters, nor plump—*zaftik*, as the Jews would say. Her hair was piled atop her head like a dragon's nest, revealing a strong neck and the briefest glimpse of a surprisingly broad back.

Some peasant stock in her lineage somewhere? He quickly brushed the ungracious thought aside. *Not all of us have to raise ourselves from the dirt to God's grace. Some are given it at birth.*

The rest of her form was disguised by draping linens and silks as the current fashion demanded, but the monk knew her waist was capable of being cinched quite tight in the fashions of other times. Her eyes, the monk also knew, were ever so slightly drooping, disguising a stern nature and stubborn resolve—especially when caring for her only son.

She turned those eyes on him now. "Yes, Father Grigori? Do you require something of me?"

The monk blinked twice rapidly, realizing he'd been staring and that perhaps "desiring her not at all" was overstating things a touch.

"Only to implore you once more to keep the bloodsuckers away," he managed to say, covering his brief awkwardness with another bow. "I feel the young tsar is so much better now that you have stopped those aspirin powders. The bruises less offensive, his energy higher."

The tsarina nodded, then sat down smoothly on the chair by the bed, a hand's space away from her sleeping son.

Rasputin took the nod as a dismissal and left the chamber quickly.

Once through the door, he slowed for just a moment. *Where is that girl with the swan's neck?* he thought. *I should like to take these unworthy feelings out on her.* He rubbed his hands together, marveling at how smooth his palms had become during his time at court. *Perhaps it is not too late to find a whip.*

The tsar sent a letter home the day after getting to the front. The tsarina opened it with shaking hands.

My Own Darling:

Again I had to leave you and the children—my home, my little nest—and I feel so sad and dejected but do not want to show it. God grant that we may not be parted for long. Do not grieve and do not worry! Knowing you well, I am afraid that you will ponder over what Misha told us the other day—that there are many dissidents in the countryside. That the Jews are fomenting revolution, and that this question will torment you in my absence. Please let it alone!

My home guard and my dragons will take care of it all.

My joy, my Sunny, my adorable little Wify, I love you and long for you terribly!

Only when I see the soldiers and sailors
do I succeed in forgetting you for a few moments—if it is possible!

God guard you! I kiss you all fondly.

Always yours,
Nicky

She wondered what she might write in return. That
Alexei was slowly recovering? That the conversations
among the various European courts were slowing down
during these days of war? That because of the war, no
Russian princess's hand could be offered to the Germans, which ruled out many of her closest cousins.

She thought, as she often did, of the last year at this
dark, cold, time, when their daughter Sonia had fallen ill
with a noise in her lungs. Remembering with an ache in
her heart, standing by Sonia's bed and watching as the
doctors put two cups on Sonia's chest. And Sonia taking
no notice, hanging like a lump in the two maids' arms.
And then watching as Sonia, wreathed in prayers, died,
but calmly and in a state of grace.

"Oh my darling child," the tsarina whispered. It was
unthinkable, a child like Sonia—so good, so kind—was
taken while others she could name—though she wouldn't,
being both a good Christian woman and a princess and
tsarina as well—lived on. Sometimes, believing in a be-
nevolent God was a stance she found hard to maintain.

Something else she would have to offer up to Father Grigori in confession.

When, this year, she herself had come down with an illness, she had felt no such calm, and little grace, but battled mightily to stay alive because she had to run the country with Nicky away. This roiling, troublesome, ungrateful country full of rebels and a culture that consisted of potatoes, hard drinks, and a peasantry that was always a problem.

A bit like England's Ireland, only without the poetry.

In her illness, the doctors had cupped her, too, and Father Grigori sent up many prayers for her safety. Her strong English and German constitution stood her in good stead, plus those prayers.

She certainly hadn't wanted to trouble Nicky with that, in the war with his terrible commanders. He would only have fretted, fearing that she, too, was dying, even if the letter was written in her own firm hand. But he always said he could not go on without her. Did not want to leave her side, ever. So why was he away on a front in an unwinnable war? Why had he left her to be a ruler in a land that didn't want her? Had never wanted her? Even after she had done so much for it.

And then she thought that she didn't really know how she would bear it if Nicholas should die before her, out on that cold, unyielding front. She only hoped he came safely home to her and that they could go to Heaven together when their time came.

Then suddenly she knew what she could actually write to him: that his filthy dragons were eating up the treasury, stinking up the castle from the ground up, and killing no Jews, which was hardly the bargain she'd expected, nor had he. She would even send a curse on the dragons in German. *Ein Fluch auf ihrem schmutzigen Drachens!* It would make him laugh and be strong.

And settling on this at last, she began to write.

"Where did you get them? Where did they come from? What do you plan for them?" Borutsch couldn't help himself; his voice trembled slightly on the last phrase.

Bronstein looked as if he were going to slap his old friend. "Quiet yourself and don't look so woman-nervous. We approach the shtetl."

Borutsch didn't answer but took another quick sip of the schnapps.

"And if you say anything about . . . about what I have just shown you . . . anything at all . . . we are both dead men. I let you in on the secret in case something happens to me. In these times, no one is safe. Once the dragons are hatched and trained, you can tell whom you like, but not until then."

Bronstein's voice trailed off, but there was a hard edge to it. Like nothing Borutsch had ever heard from him before. He took another sip of the schnapps, almost emptying the flask.

"I'll not speak of it, Lev," he said quietly. He tried for the schnapps again, but a bit of it sloshed over his shirt-front as Bronstein grabbed him roughly by the shoulders.

"You won't!" Bronstein hissed through pinched lips. "I swear to you, Borutsch. If you do. . . ."

Borutsch bristled, shook himself free, recorked the flask. "Who would I tell? And who would believe an old Jew like me? An old Jew with fewer friends in this world every day." He peered up at Bronstein and saw the manic light dim in his eyes. But still Borustch realized that he feared his friend now more than he feared any dragon. It was a sobering thought.

"I . . . I am sorry, Pinchas." Bronstein took off his glasses. Forest dirt was smeared on the lenses. He wiped them slowly on his shirt. "I don't know what came over me."

"They say that caring for dragons can make you think like one. Make you think that choosing anything but flame and ruin is a weakness."

"No, it's not that. It's. . . ." He shook his head, then put his glasses on. Went on in a firmer voice. "This world is untenable. We cannot wait upon change. Change must be brought about. And change does not happen easily." He frowned. "Or peacefully."

Borutsch took a deep breath before speaking. What he had to say seemed to sigh out of him. "The passage of time is not peaceful? And yet nothing can stand before it. Not men, not mountains. Not the hardest rock, if a river is allowed to flow across it for long enough."

"You make a good, if over-eloquent point." Bronstein sighed. "But *he* would disagree."

Borutsch frowned as if the schnapps had turned sour in his mouth. "*He* is not here."

"But he will return. When the dragons hatch. . . ."

Borutsch looked stunned. "You have shown him the eggs, too?"

"I have *told* him of the eggs."

"*If* they hatch, Pinchas. Do you know what this means?"

"Don't be an idiot. Of course I know what this means. And they *will* hatch. And I will train them."

Neither one of them had spoken above a whisper. All the Jews of the area had long been schooled in keeping their voices down. But these were sharp, harsh whispers that might just as well have been shouts.

"What do you know about training dragons?"

"What does the tsar know?"

"You are so rash, my old friend." It was as if Borutsch had never had a drop of the schnapps, for he certainly felt cold sober now. "The tsar has never trained a dragon, but his money has. And where will you, Lev Bronstein, find that kind of money?"

Bronstein laid a finger to the side of his nose and laughed. It was not a humorous sound at all. "Where Jews always find money," he said. "In other people's pockets."

Bronstein turned and looked at the morning sun. Soon it would be full day. Not that this far north in the Russias in the winter was there that much difference between day and night. All a kind of deep gray.

"And when I turn my dragons loose to destroy the tsar's armies, *he* will return."

"If *he* returns," Borutsch shouted, throwing the flask to the ground, "it will be at the head of a German column!"

"He has fought thirty years for the revolution."

"Not here he hasn't. By now, Ulyanov knows less about this land than the tsar's German wife does."

"He is Russian, not German. And he is even a quarter Jew." Bronstein sounded petulant. "And why do you not call him by the name he prefers?"

"Very well," Borutsch said. "Lenin will burn this land to the ground before saving it, just to show that his reading of Marx is more *ausgezeichnet* than mine."

Bronstein raised his hand as if to slap Borutsch, who was proud of the fact that he didn't flinch. Then, without touching his friend at all, Bronstein walked away down the hill at a sharp clip. He did not turn to see if Borutsch followed, did not even acknowledge his friend was there at all.

"You don't need to destroy the army," Borutsch called after him. "They'd come over to us eventually." Bending over, he picked up the flask. Gave it a shake. Smiled at the small, reassuring slosh it still made. Enough for one more wetting of his mouth. "Given the passage of time," he said more quietly, but Bronstein was already too far away to hear.

Borutsch wondered if he'd ever see Bronstein again. Wondered if he'd recognize him if he did. What did it matter? He was not going back to the shtetl. Not going to cower in that burrow ever again.

He flung the flask away angrily and watched as it rolled a bit down the hill, leaving a strange trail in the snow.

"Not going to drink any more cheap schnapps, either. If there's going to be a war with all those dragons," he said to himself, "I will leave *me* out of it." He'd already started the negotiations to sell his companies. He'd take his family to Europe, maybe even to Berlin. It would certainly be safer than here when the dragon smoke began to cover all of the land. When the tsar and his family would be as much at risk as the Jews.

He looked back at the hills they'd just walked, behind which the eggs lay buried and ready to hatch.

Each a little bomb, he thought, then shivered. They were not little at all. Each was bigger than a bomb and could deliver its blasts over and over and over again until the world truly was in flames.

He nodded to himself. Better to leave sooner than later. If he could find any paper in his house, which, luckily, had only lost a barn and his wife's two cows, he would write to his lawyer in Germany and send it by messenger in the morning.

I took the stairs two at a time. Coming around the corner on the floor where the apartments were situated, I told myself that it no longer mattered who was there with Ninotchka—cookboy or prince. Out he will go.

And I shall lock her in her room.

Though I rarely gave orders, she knew when she had to listen to me. It was in the voice, of course.

After I lock her in, I will send out invitations to those I already know are against the monk.

I checked my face in a hall mirror. Damn, my face looked grim, nearly growling. But I didn't feel grim. I felt elated, counting the conspirators on my fingers as I strode down the hall. The archbishop of course, because Rasputin had called rather too often for the peasants to forgo the clergy and find God in their own hearts. The head of the army, because of the monk's anti-war passions. To his credit, the tsar did not think highly of the madman's stance, and when Rasputin expressed a desire to bless the troops at the front, Nicholas had roared out, "Put a foot on that sacred ground, and I will have you hanged at once." I had never heard him so decisive and magnificent before or—alas—since.

I shall also ask Prince Yusupov and Grand Duke Pavlovich, who have their own reasons for hating him. And one or two others. But then another thought occurred to me. *Too many in a conspiracy will make it fail. We need not a net but a hammer, for as the old babushkas like to say, "A hammer shatters glass but forges steel." And this operation needs both the shattered glass and the steel.*

I already knew that my old friend Vladimir would be by my side. Vladimir had called Rasputin out in the Duma, saying in a passionate speech that the monk had taken the tsar's ministers firmly in hand, saying brilliantly that the ministers "have been turned into marionettes."

What a fine figure of speech! I hardly knew he had it in him. A good man with a pistol, though. I counted on that pistol.

But was one pistol enough? The peasants believed Rasputin unkillable. And no one doubted the story of that slattern who tried to gut him with a filleting knife, calling him the antichrist. She had missed her opportunity, alas for Russia. Yes, her knife slid through his soft belly, and he stood before her with his entrails spilling out. But some local doctor pushed the tangled mess back in the empty cavity and sewed him up again.

"Or so they say. So they say." I was muttering to myself now. With the mad monk, it's difficult to know how much is true and how much is story.

Oh yes, he might be the very devil to kill.

And realizing that I'd made a joke—I entered the apartment, giggling.

Ninotchka was working on her sewing in the alcove. Two women friends, the delightful Masha and the despicable tart-tongued Dasha, plus the maid who cleaned up the place, were walking around her, gabbling like geese. Ninotchka looked up, her blond hair framing that perfect, heart-shaped face.

"A joke, my darling?" she asked.

"A joke," I agreed, "but not one a man can share with his adorable wife." I cupped her chin with my right hand.

She wrinkled her nose. "You stink, my love. What *is* that smell?"

I'd forgotten to wash the stench of dragon off my hands.

"It is nothing. I was talking to the horses that pull our carriage, reminding them of what sweet cargo they will have aboard tonight."

"Tonight?" The look in her eyes forgave me the stench. It was not yet the start of the Season, and she had been growing feverish for some fun.

I planned to take her to the Mariinsky Theatre and dinner afterwards. And she would reward me later, of that I was certain.

"I have planned a special treat out for us. It will be a surprise," I said. It was amazing how easily the lie came out. "But now I have business," I added. "I beg you to go to your rooms. You and your women."

"Government business?" she asked sweetly, but I knew better than to hint now. She was simply trying to discover some bit of gossip she could sell to the highest bidder. After all, I alone could not keep her in jewels.

Later in bed, I will sleepily let out a minor secret. Not this one, of course. I am a patriot, after all. I serve the tsar. Even though the tsar has not lately served me and mine at all.

I smiled back. "Very definitely government business."

As soon as Ninotchka and the women went into her room, and the maid went on to the next apartments to clean them, I locked her door from the outside.

Let them make of that what they will, I thought, though knowing it was government business would keep them from complaining.

Then I sat at my desk and wrote the letters, taking a great deal of time on the initial one until I was satisfied with the way I had suggested but never actually said what the reason for the meeting was.

Then I sent for Nikita to deliver the letters and to make a reservation at the Mariinsky and Chez Galouise, the finest French restaurant in the city, for their last sitting. I knew I could trust Semyon completely, thinking, *He, at least, would never shop me to my enemies. After all, I have saved his life upon three separate occasions. That kind of loyalty is what distinguishes a man from a woman.*

The mad monk lay in a pile of flesh and blankets and was nearly content. He'd been unable to find the swan-necked lady-in-waiting but had made do with a fleshy and mostly willing tradesman's daughter who had a head of brilliant red curls and, alas, nothing inside it. A quick tumble had nearly knocked the unworthy thoughts of the tsarina out of his head, and when they returned a few minutes later, he merely ploughed the young woman again. She hadn't the energy to protest by then. He was naked except for a silver cross on a braided chain that he never removed, for it was charmed. While he wore it, he could not be killed by the hand of man. God had charmed it, and God had told him of it.

And God is good. He has raised me up from nothing. He has fulfilled my every dream. He has put me next to the tsar so I can whisper His wisdom into the ears of power.

But he knew that great care was needed now. Though God was known to reward His faithful, He was also known to punish those who begin to expect those rewards. Who think they deserve them.

Pride and Hubris. Rasputin named the twin devils that he knew he was especially susceptible to. *They have brought down many a devoted man. I must ensure I am not another.*

He swore that he would do only God's work. Sing only His praises. That the women, the power, they meant nothing to him. Merely trifles compared to power and glory of a great and generous God.

He felt so enflamed with God's love that he nearly rode the girl a third time. But he recognized it as a trap. The first two dalliances had served a purpose; a third would have been for his own indulgence.

And I exist only to serve God.

He stood and stretched, enjoying the play of the many cold drafts in the tradesman's house across his naked body, then slipped back into his robe. The rough cloth scraped him in places so recently overused, but the discomfort only reminded him of his duty.

Pain, discomfort, hardship. I will suffer them all and gladly for the greater glory of God.

He aimed a beatific smile at the girl, but she had slipped into a twitchy slumber. She would not see him leave.

And she will not see me ever again. She has served her purpose. God's purpose, he reminded himself. He left a gold coin on the pillow. She would know what that meant. It was surely more than she expected, though perhaps less than she had hoped.

As he left the tradesman's house, a cold wind sliced off

the Neva and hit him full in the face. He didn't feel it. He felt only the golden warmth of God's glorious love.

Spring would surely break in Russia like the smiles of women Bronstein had known: cautious, cold, and a long time coming.

Now, however, they were in the deepest part of the winter. Snow lay indifferently on the ground as if it knew it still had months of discomfort to visit on the people, rich and poor alike. *But,* Bronstein told himself, *on the poor even more.* The peasants, at the bottom of the heap, might even have to tear the thatch from their roofs to feed the livestock if things got much worse.

He'd visited the eggs a dozen more times, each visit going by a different route, from every conceivable compass point. Always checking for followers. Always looking for footprints not his own. And always carefully brushing away his back-trail. He spent hours with the eggs, squatting in the cold, snowy field, and talking out his plans as if the dragons could hear him through the tough elastic shells. He had no one else to tell. Borutsch had fled to Berlin, and Bronstein feared the old man had spilled his secret before leaving. But as he—so far at least—had not spotted anyone close by, and the eggs had not been disturbed, he was reasonably certain that even if Borutsch had spoken of what he'd seen, people would have thought him deranged. An old man at the end of his life muttering about dragons.

But this time. . . .

Bronstein saw something was wrong as soon as he spotted the lightning-split pine. The ground beneath it was torn up, the leaves scattered. Running up to the tree, he gaped in horror at a hole in the ground.

It was completely devoid of eggs.

Mein Gott und Marx, he swore in silent German. *The tsar's men have found them. And they will have broomed away their steps even as I. . . .*

Whether it was Borutsch's fault or his own carelessness, there was no time to tear his hair or weep uncontrollably, no time for recriminations. He simply had to flee.

Perhaps I can join Borutsch in Berlin. If he'll have me.

Bronstein turned to run but was stopped cold by a rustling sound in the brush behind him.

Soldiers! he thought desperately. Reaching into his pocket and pulling out a small pistol he'd taken to carrying, he waved it at his unseen enemies before realizing how useless it would be against what sounded like an entire company of soldiers.

Swiveling his head from side to side as more rustling came from all around him, he came to a grim decision.

So this is how it ends.

The gun shook as he raised it to his temple.

"Long live the revolution!" he shouted, then winced. *Oh, to not have died with a cliché on my lips.*

His finger tightened on the trigger, then stopped just short of firing as he realized how truly stupid he was.

A dragon the size of a newborn lamb—and just as unsteady on its feet—pushed through the bushes and into view.

"*Gevalt*," he breathed.

The dragon emitted a sound somewhere between a mew and a hiss and wobbled directly up to Bronstein, who took an involuntary step back. The creature was fearsome to look at even as a hatchling, all leathery hide and oversized bat wings. Its eyes were the gold of a wolf, though still cloudy from the albumin that coated its skin and made it glisten in the thin forest light.

Bronstein wondered wildly if the eyes would stay that color or change, as babies' eyes do. He'd heard the tsar's dragons had eyes like shrouds. Of course the man who told him that could have been exaggerating for effect. And though the pronounced teeth that gave the adult dragons their sinister appearance had yet to grow in, the egg-tooth at the tip of the little dragonling's beak looked sharp enough to kill if called upon. And the claws that scritch-scratched through the sticks and leaves even now looked as though they could easily gut a cow.

But Bronstein quickly remembered Lenin's advice:

Dragons, like the bourgeois, respect only power. When they are fresh-hatched, you must be the only power they know.

He pocketed the pistol that he still held stupidly to his head and stepped forward, putting both hands on the dragon's moist skin.

"Down, beast," he said firmly, pressing down. The beast collapsed on its side, mewling piteously. Grabbing a handful of dead leaves from the trees, Bronstein began scraping and scrubbing, cleaning the egg slime from the dragon's skin, talking the whole time. "Down, beast," he said sternly. "Stay still, monster."

More dragons wandered out of the brush, attracted, no doubt, by the sound of his voice.

Perhaps, Bronstein thought, *they really* could *hear me through their shells these last few months.* Whether true or not, he was glad he'd spoken to them all that while.

"Down," he bade the new dragons, and they, too, obeyed.

As he scraped and scrubbed, Bronstein could see the dragon's skin color emerging from the albumin slime. It was red, not black.

Red like hearth fire, red like heart's blood, red like revolution.

Somehow, that was comforting.

The mad monk had heard talk of dragons. Of course he'd often heard talk of dragons. But this time there was something different in the tenor of the conversations, and he was always alert to changes in gossip.

Gossip is the beginning of history. Someone not alert to it could let history slide past them.

This particular bit of dragon gossip had something to do with a red terror, which was odd, since the tsar's dragons were black. But when his sources were pressed further—a kitchen maid, a boot boy, the man-boy who exercised the tsar's dogs and slept with them as well—they could say nothing more than that. And the dog boy—whose vocabulary was interspersed with dog grunts and growls—sounded perfectly terrified when he spoke to Rasputin about it. Or rather, he tried to speak. He ended up howling like one of his charges instead.

Red terror! Rasputin tried to imagine what they meant, his hands wrangling together. It could mean nothing or everything. It could have nothing to do with dragons at all and everything to do with assassination attempts. A palace was the perfect place for such plots. Like a dish of stew left on the stove too many days, there was a stink about it.

But if there was a plot, he would know it. He would master it. He would use it for his own good.

"Find me more about this red terror," he whispered to the kitchen maid, a skinny little thing, with a crooked nose. "And we will talk of marriage." That he was already married mattered not a bit. He would find her a mate, someone who would lift her out of the kitchen, and she knew it.

"Find me more about this red terror," he told the boot boy, "and I shall make sure you rise to footman." It was his little joke, that. The boy was not smart enough for the job he already had. But there were always ways to make the boy think he'd tried.

He said nothing more to the dog's keeper. As his old mother used to tell him: *A spoken word is not a sparrow. Once it flies out, you can't catch it.* He knew the dog boy spoke in his sleep, his hands and feet scrabbling on the rushes the way his hounds did when they dreamed. Everybody listened in.

The truth that peasants speak is not the same as the truth the powerful know. Having been one and become the other, Rasputin knew this better than most. He wrung his hands once more. "Find me more about this red terror," he muttered to no one in particular.

But even as he asked, he drew in upon himself, becoming moody, cautious, worried. Walking alone by the frozen River Neva, he tried to puzzle through all he'd heard. It was as if the world was sending him messages in code. He asked his secretary Simanovich for paper and wrote a letter to the tsar telling him of the signs and warning him, too.

The words scratched out onto the page, but while they made perfect sense to Rasputin, schooled as he was in the meanings of magic, he knew he would need more for the tsar to act on than what was offered therein. So Rasputin did not send the letter. Not yet. Once he found out all about this red terror, he would personally hand the letter to the tsar and reap his reward.

It was past time for his visit with the tsar's son, and the boy was restless. He snapped at Rasputin, saying, "You are late. No one is late coming to me."

The monk made a *tch* with his tongue, as he would to a badly trained dog, and the boy immediately came to heel. "I was looking for a special treat, little tsar," he said smoothly. Not that he had any such treat, nor could he afford something the boy did not already have. But it worked.

"What? What?" Alexei asked, eager as always.

"We are going to go down to see the dragons, and on

the way, I have a very special tale to tell you about dragons," Rasputin said.

"Is it about the tsar's dragons?" Alexei asked, slipping his hand in the monk's.

"It is about. . . ." Rasputin thought quickly, remembering the tales he'd heard from the old women in his native village. "About *a* dragon. But not your father's."

"Oh." The boy sounded disappointed. "I don't wish to hear about *Chinese* dragons."

"But these are Russian dragons."

"There are no Russian dragons that aren't my father's," Alexei said imperiously.

"Not anymore," Rasputin said, mysteriously.

"Tell me, tell me," Alexei begged, not a royal command but a boy's plea.

"As we walk along," Rasputin said, knowing the walk would be good for the boy.

The boy looked up expectantly yet silently, so Rasputin began the tale.

"There once was a snake that lived a hundred years, and so turned into a dragon. This was in Russia, not China, so it turned into a giant dragon, not a small wyrm like we have now."

"My father's dragons aren't small!" Alexei said petulantly. "They are the tsar's dragons, which means they are the biggest—"

Rasputin smiled down at him. "Of course not," he agreed, because disagreeing openly with royalty was never a good idea. "But compared to the Russian dragons of old? Tiny things." He waited until the boy nodded in agreement before continuing. "After one hundred years a snake, this dragon was wild, as well. Untamable. He razed villages. Burnt whole provinces to ash."

"Was there no tsar to stop him?"

"Of course there was! Your grandfather's grandfather's grandfather was tsar," Rasputin said, having no idea if it was true. "He rode out to slay the dragon."

Alexei made as if to speak, but Rasputin held his hand up to stop him. "I will never finish if you keep interrupting, my prince. The tsar rode out in his shining armor and, avoiding the flames, plunged his great sword deep into the beast's chest."

The boy couldn't help himself. He burst out, "He killed the dragon!"

Rasputin smiled. "No. Because the dragon was not only large and fierce but clever, as well. He had taken out his heart and hidden it far away, where none could find it. Or so he thought."

"Did the tsar find the dragon's heart? Did he save the land?"

Rasputin laughed and scooped up the young prince— but gently. They neared the entrance to the barns. "Of course, he did." And since they were at the barns now, added, "But that is a story for another day."

They went down to the barns, but the dragons were sleeping, or so the barn boys said. And even a tsar's son—

warned Rasputin—dare not wake them. They saw only the tops of the dragons' sleeping heads. Alexei was more than satisfied.

Rasputin was relieved.

The tsarina was waiting for them impatiently, her ladies buzzing around her like bees around their queen. The monk and the boy were an hour past the doctor's appointment, which had to be rescheduled for after the evening meal. The tsarina was not amused.

"Insufferable. . . ." she began, tapping the gold watch pinned to the bib of her dress, but then she saw Alexei's face. It was suffused with excitement, not its usual bleached complexion with fever spots on either cheek. She said more quietly, "My dear son, where have you and the good father been?"

"To the dragons, Mama," he said, adding quickly, "and I learned about my great-great so many times great grandfather, who saved the land from a great dragon. He was so heroic. I want to be like that."

She turned to Rasputin, "What nonsense have you been filling his head with?"

"Heroism in a princeling is never nonsense, Majesty," he answered solemnly. "And it gives him much to live up to, don't you think?" He gazed down at the boy fondly, his hand familiarly on the child's head.

"And look, Mama," Alexei said, holding something up to her in an unusually grimy hand. "A strand of hair from one dragon's head. I should like it in a locket to wear beneath my shirt always, to remind me to be brave."

"Remind you. . . ." She looked at her child, who was already braver than she had ever had to be. She hoped he never had to have more courage than to face the doctors with their little probes. Or the sudden losses of blood that came with the terrible disease her ancestors had gifted him with. And the swollen limbs and bruises as large as summer plums.

"Of course," she said, careful not to shudder as she held out her hand for the dark hank of hair, before handing it quickly to one of her ladies. "Kita will have it set in a golden locket for you, a masculine locket. Yes?"

Kita curtseyed and held out her hand for the disgusting piece of hair. She, poor thing, had no ability to control her shudder at the touch. The tsarina gave her a look that might have frozen a dragon in its tracks.

Then the tsarina turned. "Such lateness will not happen again, Father Grigori," she said to Rasputin. But her voice was warm enough to tell him he had been forgiven.

He put his hand over his heart and bowed, gifting her with that wonderful smile, and a wink for Alexei.

It was an unorthodox thing for a priest to do. But Alexei looked so happy with his whole adventure, the tsarina didn't have the heart to scold further.

But as the evening wore on, she thought more and more about her precious Alexei being brought down to the dragon pens. It really was the height of arrogance and irresponsibility for the monk to expose him to such beasts. For beasts they were, and useless beasts as well, now that they never seemed to find any Jews to kill. How could Rasputin—her beloved Rasputin—betray her like this?

She didn't know the answer to that, of course, but she knew who would.

Nicky, my darling, Nicky.

She would tell him of the monk's overreach when he returned from the front. He would tell her what they should do.

Bronstein was exhausted. The dragons were needy, greedy things, big as cattle now but with the manners of kittens. Soon that last would change. He had to train them before then.

And they were so endlessly hungry!

He spent most of his days gathering food for them: scraps from the fishmongers, offal from the slaughterhouse, bones from the butcher. Even chickens, alive or newly dead. His excuses were varied: hounds to feed, dinner parties, food for the poor. A few of the butchers may have guessed at the truth, but it was too outlandish an idea to be believed. *A Jew raising dragons? Now tell us about the German who hugged his children, or the Cossack who hated vodka.* So what if it was the only answer that made sense? It still made no sense at all. So to stamp out any last doubts, Bronstein had to make some of that true so as not to start even more rumors. He made sure to be seen throwing parties and feeding the poor—but never so much that there wasn't anything left over for his dragons. And once he was even seen running a pack of hounds—stolen of course, and fed to the dragons after—

like some English lord a-hunting. It seemed endless, the subterfuge, the drudgery, the fear, though he knew it was not.

The dragons honked at him when he returned and butted him with their bullet-shaped heads. After feeding them, he had to fix the fences they'd trampled or burned and collect the larger dragons who had wandered off. He had a few boys from the village who helped him, but it seemed that the only ones trustworthy enough to recruit were mostly useless when it came to the actual work.

And there was so much work!

Bronstein was not afraid of work. But this wasn't his *kind* of work. Writing, editing, running a newspaper—he could do that for sixteen, eighteen hours a day. But this was peasant's labor, all sweat and slop, so much heaving, hoisting, and hosing down . . . it was really too much!

But help is on its way, he thought, taking out his watch and checking it. *In fact, I have just enough time to clean myself up before meeting their train.*

Bronstein rode to the station in his second-best suit, his beard trimmed, his eyeglasses wiped clean as laboratory glass. When he reached the city, and the smell of coal and crowds hit him, he suddenly realized how much he missed the big cities of Europe.

I was happy in Vienna. In London.

He would have stayed in either place, writing his stories, running his newspapers. Stayed but for the lure of dragons and the power they brought.

He wondered if there was something to what Borutsch had said. That men who stayed too long around dragons started to think like them.

A man would surely know if he had changed so much.

But he was not so sure he remembered what he'd been like before Siberia. Before leaving his wife and child behind to ride a hay wagon through the snow to freedom. If he hadn't believed the stories of a lost brood of eggs that old Chinese man had drunkenly spilled, would he even now be living in such a harmonious and pastoral—if a bit frozen—land?

The screech of the steam train braking brought him out of his reverie, the cloud of smoke not unlike that which dribbled out of the young dragons' noses.

He realized with sudden clarity that it didn't matter what choices he might or might not have made. Lenin's lieutenants had arrived, and it was time to be about the work of the people.

I had been thinking about the plan all day. All week. Weeks now. Fining it down, refining it. And now I admitted what I had not dared before—that it was a masterful plan. Especially since my presence would be necessary for its execution.

Execution! I giggled at the play on words, and Ninotchka glanced at me coldly. Her face was as powdered as her hair, which suddenly made her look surprisingly old. I giggled again. Old and haggard. While I felt young, virile and . . . well, alive! I wondered how I'd never before noticed how old cosmetics can make some women look.

"Did I say something to amuse you, my husband?" Her voice was disinterested, uncaring, the word *husband* ashes in her mouth.

Thinking back over the past few weeks, I realized she had grown increasingly distant.

Possibly, I thought, *due to my spending long hours pulling together the threads of my plot into a web that Rasputin cannot possibly escape. He can neither refuse the invitation to dinner from a noble nor survive the meal I've planned for him.*

I suppressed another giggle. *And I will be there. Nothing can keep me from seeing the look on his arrogant face as he realizes I am the architect of his destruction. Did he think he could cuckold me without a response?*

For a moment, I turned my back on Ninotchka to regain control of my face, my shaking hands.

When I was once again facing her, she looked astonished, eyes wide, as if she had guessed. *But of course she could not have guessed. I am the perfect keeper of secrets. I have destroyed better men than Rasputin in the service of the tsar. Occasionally, I have even killed them on the tsar's orders. Not with my own hands, of course. Never my own hands.*

Knowing the right men for such tasks was my job. A word in the right ear, a bit of money passed carefully, a hostage to keep the killer in line. I am very good at what I do. If the monk's mad eyes seemed to look through me whenever we met in the palace halls—well, that would not last long. Soon I would see them closed forever.

"No," I said to Ninotchka. "You have not the wit." Having planned to dispose of Rasputin on her behalf, I now was suddenly tired of her constant sniping. *A man does what he must to protect his spouse and thereby his own good name. And—if she was especially unappreciative of his efforts—he may very well find himself a new wife who was.*

I looked deeply into her eyes, reminding her who was master here, and emphasized each word. "No, you say *nothing* that amuses me these days."

Taking pleasure in a second, even wider look of surprise that she gave me, I spun smartly on my heels and quick-marched from the sitting room, boots tip-tapping a message to her with every step.

"After all," I whispered to the empty hall, "I have a group of aristos to shore up. Just in case . . . just in case the poisoned borscht doesn't kill the monk on the first go-round. Unlikely, but one never knows."

To survive in this world, one must always make backup plans to one's backup plans.

That thought was followed immediately by an even pleasanter one.

I must look to the ladies at court. It would be good to have someone in waiting when it is time for Ninotchka to go.

The tsarina had sent a note to Rasputin in French. She'd never quite mastered the Cyrillic. Her elegant handwriting hid the meanness of the message. He assumed she meant it to. He got the gist of the beginning but the rest was too difficult for him.

The tsarevitch Alexei will not be able to see you this week.

The tsarina had even left off her signature, which made it unclear if she had written it herself or had someone else do it for her. Possibly something the tsar had dictated. He could not believe the tsarina—who was so devoted to him and so thankful for his tender care of her son—he could not believe she would ever cut him off like this. But the tsar, perhaps. He had been cold to the monk since his return from the front.

Of course he can treat me any way he wishes. He is the tsar. And the monk would never deign to suggest how God's ruler on Earth should comport himself. *But God may judge him harshly if he mistreats such a valuable messenger of His Word as myself.*

He needed a much better read of the letter to determine who was behind his exile from the tsarina's good graces. Since his French was—at best—simple phrases, he would need to find someone else to read the message for him so that he understood it completely. He settled at last on the beautiful Ninotchka, the wife of that silly bureaucrat whose name always escaped him.

She read it eagerly, her small breasts heaving up and down as she translated, which he took for a sign that she might be willing for a tumble in her capacious bed.

Her voice was light, a bit silly, but silliness had never put him off.

"The tsarevitch Alexei. . . ," she read, "will not be able to see you this week. The doctors have agreed he needs full rest from his latest bad turn. . . . A nursing staff is in charge. You excite his blood too much, dear Father Grigori. Those trips—that started with the visit to the dragons—must be ended. All other visitations with him will be chaperoned. It is the tsar's wish, and mine as well."

Ninotchka finished, bit her lower lip prettily.

"This is just between us, my child," Rasputin said and took the paper back from her, careful not to touch her hand. He suddenly dared not let a spark travel between them. There were too many other women about, and it was too dangerous. Besides, he was stunned by the coldness in the tsarina's letter, which the "dear Father Grigori" did nothing to disguise. He had to think about what it meant. And who had written it.

So he gave Ninotchka one of his well-practiced smoldering looks and departed with the note crumpled in his hand.

Back in his rooms, he smoothed out the note with a warm iron and read it himself with much difficulty, hearing it in Ninotchka's light voice as he did, thinking about the delightful afternoon tryst he'd been forced to forgo. The note's contents did not improve with a second reading.

Had he overplayed his cards? He was usually good at such games. A champion at *Eralash* and *Siberian Vint*. But politics had been the game he played best. 'Til now.

He repeated it out loud and bitterly. "'Til now."

The red dragons were restless that evening in their burrows, snapping at their keepers and tugging at their leads. Bronstein tried to keep them in line—he was the only one they really listened to—but even he was having trouble with them that night. Others might have thought to use a whip. A cat-o-nine tails was always close to hand, and a buggy whip as well. But Bronstein eschewed the rougher methods, leading the dragons with a firm hand and a firmer voice. Usually it worked.

"Why do they act this way?"

"And why do you not stop them? You have a whip."

The speakers were Koba and Kamo, two middlemen sent by Lenin to oversee the training of the beasts. Or the "Red Terror," as Lenin had dubbed them. That was so like him, trusting no one. Not even his own handpicked men. He'd told them nothing beside the fact that they would be underground. They'd assumed they were to be spies. And they were, of a sort.

Though they looked quite different—one strikingly handsome with windswept hair and a disarming smile, the other a frog-eyed caricature of a typical Georgian peasant—Bronstein couldn't tell Koba and Kamo apart. Something in their manner made them identical in his mind: arrogance compounded by . . . by. . . . He couldn't quite put his finger on it.

"The dragons are bred to the sky," he said archly, "and this stay underground irks them. To beat them will only make them tenser, more dangerous."

"Then why even have the whips?" asked perhaps-Kamo.

"It makes *me* calmer," Bronstein told them, with a bit of self-deprecating humor in his voice. That neither of them laughed was another dark tick against them.

Bronstein fixed one of them—the handsome one—with a glare. *Koba, maybe.* "And you may try to stop them if you wish." He realized he was trying to train the two men as he trained the dragons, with a combination of strength and cozening.

Maybe-Koba looked at the dragons for a moment as if considering it. He didn't look hopeful. But he didn't look frightened, either.

Bronstein snapped imaginary fingers. That was it! Arrogance compounded by blind stupidity. They didn't know enough to be afraid of the dragons. Or of Lenin. *Or*—he considered carefully—*of him*. The dragons were smarter, but Koba and Kamo served a different master. He wondered if that made the difference.

"My apologies, Comrade Bronstein," Maybe-Koba said, his voice flat.

110

He didn't sound sorry. *The man is an entire library of negatives*, Bronstein thought.

Maybe-Koba went on. "We shall let you return to your work. Comrade Lenin will be here within days. Then we shall release the Red Terror to cleanse this land. Lenin has said it, and now I understand what he means. Come, Kamo."

Koba it is, then, Bronstein thought, adding aloud, "Cleanse it of what? Of Russians?"

Bronstein knew that Koba—or maybe Kamo, *does it really matter?*—had been a Georgian Social Democrat and nationalist and some whispered a separatist before joining Lenin to free the entire working class. Some said Koba—or maybe Kamo—still was. The fractures in the revolution made Bronstein's head hurt. Without realizing it, he rubbed his cigarette-stained fingers against his temples.

Koba stared at Bronstein with no trace of emotion on his face. "Of the tsar. And his followers. Are you feeling ill?" As if a headache dropped Bronstein even further in his estimation.

Despite his flowing hair and soft brown eyes, there was something hard about Koba, Bronstein decided, like his innards were made of stone or steel rather than flesh and blood. But the men followed him. Followed him without question. Not that the men who followed Koba asked a lot of questions. They might fight for the workers, but they looked like idlers and ne'er-do-wells to Bronstein.

Are these the professional revolutionaries Lenin envisioned when he split the party?

Bronstein decided that *ne'er-do-well* was too kind a term to apply to these fellows. They looked more like thieves and murderers, and most likely anti-Semites.

But maybe those were the kind of men you needed to win a revolution.

He remembered when that was a philosophical question. Back in England, when he and Lenin and Borutsch all worked at *Iskra*, the revolutionary paper. He'd sided with Borutsch then, averring that education, enlightenment, and just a touch of propaganda would turn the entire working class to the revolution's side. There'd be no need for war or violence, and certainly no need for dragons.

But that was before his forced *education* in Siberia. Before his *enlightenment* on Bloody Sunday. He knew now that revolution was a dirty business. A bloody business.

He grunted. So was tyranny.

"I will provide the dragons, Koba, and you provide the men. Together we will *free* this land."

"Comrade Lenin will be here soon. He will say if there will be freedom or not."

Bronstein shuddered, but only inwardly. Outwardly, he was ice. Freedom was not a bargaining chip. It was the sole purpose of a revolution. *What on Earth is Lenin thinking?*

Is he mad?

He swore to himself that his dragons would make a meal of Koba and Kamo if they tried to corrupt the revolution. He would chop them into bite-sized pieces himself. He imagined feeding the dragons from a trough full of Koba-Kamo bits while Lenin asked him where his lieutenants had gotten to.

"Why Comrade Lenin, I have no idea. But I never trusted them. Never believed they were truly committed to the revolution."

"Be sure his dragons are ready," Koba said, interrupting his reverie. The Georgian turned sharply and headed up the tunnel with Kamo right behind.

His dragons? Do they mean *Lenin's* dragons? Bronstein's hand twitched. *They are* not *Lenin's dragons! Who stayed up nights with the beasts? Who imprinted them? Who fed them by hand?*

How he would have loved to wring the necks of these interlopers. He briefly revisited his trough fantasy, but it was no longer a comfort. Just made him think again about Borustch's warning.

Did I have these violent fantasies before I became a dragon-keeper?

He was an intellectual, a writer. Not a bully. Not a murderer. He shuddered, trying to turn his mind away from blood and violence. But one of the dragons chose that moment to bite off the finger of a young man who was grooming him, and Bronstein had to run and help retrieve the digit from the dragon's mouth before it was swallowed.

Lenin will be here soon, he thought, smacking the dragon on the top of its stone-hard head until it opened its mouth. The finger was still on the creature's tongue. For a second he stared at it, as if it were a piece of meat. Then he snatched it out before the dragon's jaws snapped shut.

He tossed it to its bleeding and howling former owner before wiping his hands on his shirt. Perhaps the doctor could sew it back on. Perhaps not.

Fingers, dragons, revolutionaries, his thoughts cascaded. *There's no way we'll be ready in time.*

And yet they had to be.

Rasputin looked in the great mirror and saw the effects of two weeks of self-administered flagellations and hours of kneeling in prayer. He decided he was wolf-lean and wild-eyed, but still handsome. Still, what did that matter when he had never discovered who it was who had engineered his exile, for exile it was, weeks without a summons to attend the tsarina or her son, or even another note. He had finally turned to God to explain the silence from the palace and for the first time in his life had received naught but silence from Him as well.

He had howled in his apartments as the cat bit into his back, threw prayers skyward at the top of his lungs, but still nothing.

Then finally today, a letter. An invitation. But not from the tsarina. . . .

He grimaced at his reflection, his teeth ice-white compared to the smiles of the peasants he had known. Brushing his fingers through his beard, he loosened a few scattered bits of bread stuck in the hairs.

Always go to a dinner full, his mother had warned. *The*

hungry man looks like a greedy man. He had no desire to look greedy to these men. Hard, yes. Powerful, definitely. But not greedy. A greedy man is considered prey.

An intimate supper in Prince Yusupov's house in Petrograd at 9, the invitation had read.

Perhaps it was to be the end of his estrangement from the royal family. Or at least a new way back in.

He knew that Yusupov's palace was a magnificent building on the Moika, though he'd never before been invited to dine there. He and the prince had parted company some time ago; he never quite understood why.

He'd heard in the gossipy servants' quarters that the prince's great hall had six equal sides, each guarded by a large wooden door. He wondered which door he was to enter through, which door he would leave from. These things mattered.

"Let me go through the door to Heaven," he muttered to God, part of an ongoing conversation about his new place in the world. "Let me enter and leave in glory."

His grimace turned to a beatific smile as he felt more than heard the Word of God.

Yes. Glory.

That morning, after receiving the invitation, he'd played the tarot cards and saw that six would be a number of change for him. He was ready. But then, he was *always* ready. Didn't he always wear his charm against death by a man's hand? He never took it off, not in the bathhouse, not in bed. A man with so many enemies had to be prepared. He was delighted that Prince Yusupov was no longer one of them.

And really, Yusupov is but a boy in man's clothing.

Rasputin was pleased to be in God's grace again. He knew that Yusupov had gotten his place at court through marriage. *He needs me now more than I need him.* Still, going to the palace would give him the opportunity to meet the prince's wife, the tsar's lovely niece, Irina of the piercing eyes. He had heard many things about her and all of them wonderful. Rasputin had not yet had the pleasure. *Well, it would be her pleasure, too.*

That dog Vladimir Purishkevich was picking him up in a state automobile. He supposed he could abide the man for the time it took to drive to the prince's palace. Then he would turn his back and mesmerize the princess right there, in front of her husband and his friends. They'd make a game of it. But it would not be a game. Not entirely.

Really, he felt, *no one can stop me now.* God had returned to him. Like Isaac or Job or Abraham, he had passed the trials God had set before him. With his whip and his prayers, he had triumphed, and God had returned and given him this gift. This passage back into grace. He began to laugh. It began softly but soon rose to almost maniacal heights.

A knock on the door recalled him to himself.

"Father Grigori," his man asked. "Are you choking?"

"I am laughing, imbecile," he answered, but gently,

because the man had been with him since the days of the flagellants, and a man of such fervid loyalty could not be found elsewhere. Or bought.

The door opened, and his man shuffled in, hunched and slow. "My . . . apologies, Father Grigori," he stuttered. "But I have news." He hauled one of the dragon boys in with him. The boy had a nose clotted with snot, and he sniveled.

Rasputin waited, but the man said nothing more. *He really is an imbecile*, the mad monk thought. The boy said nothing, either. Waiting, Rasputin assumed, for a sign from his elders. And betters.

Raising an eyebrow, Rasputin finally cued the man. "And this news is. . . ?"

It was the boy who spoke, trembling, the clot loosened, snot running down towards his mouth. "Your holiness, I . . . I have found the Red Terror."

Rasputin stood and waved them fully inside his chambers, handing the sniveling boy a clean handkerchief to wipe his nose with, since he seemed disinclined to use his own sleeve.

"Quickly, quickly," Father Grigori said, trying to balance his voice between anger—which might silence the stupid boy forever—and over-eagerness, which might push the boy to augment his report or simply make up parts of the tale. "Come in, where we will not be over-heard, and tell me everything."

"It is about dragons, red dragons, and there is a man called Lenin who will free them, but he will not be here until the month's end. Three days from now. When the moon is full. Only when he comes. . . ."

The boy babbled on for a few more minutes but said nothing else of interest. It didn't matter. Rasputin knew all he needed to now.

Dragons, he thought. *Red dragons.* The news was yet another sign of the love that the Lord God had for his most worthy of servants.

"Heat up water for my bath," Rasputin said to his man, the boy already forgotten in his haste. "Lay out a clean outfit. This evening I dine with princes."

But first I will bring this news to the tsar. It is sure to get me back into his good graces.

Lying in the copper tub filled to the brim with steaming water, Rasputin gave thought to the evening ahead. In his mind, it had become a celebration instead of a ploy to insinuate himself back into the palace.

There is no need now! The information he now possessed was too valuable. *An upstart Marxist has gotten his hands on some dragons? That is news that could make a man's fortune.*

Rasputin decided that he would not only bring this news to the tsar but also help him with stratagems to destroy the red dragons and trap the revolutionary leader.

And then *I shall go to dinner!*

How he would charm them all. Possibly one or more of the tsar's nubile young daughters would be at the dinner. None of them married yet. Maybe the youngest, Anastasia, an untouched blossom.

He sank for a moment below the water, feeling it wash through his hair. Felt it healing the recent scores from the whip.

Dragons. Red dragons. Thank you, dear Lord.

The tsarina looked over each of her daughters carefully. They were in their party frocks, and each one was more beautiful than the last.

Like princesses in one of the dear tales the Brothers Grimm set down, she thought. *Though thank the good Lord they have not had to go through great perils.*

Alexei looked well, too. The days of rest, the return of the doctor's strict regimen, seemed to help. Nicky had been right about that. Father Grigori did so shake the poor child up.

Turning to her youngest daughter, she snapped, "Stand straight, Anastasia. And fix your ribbon. A grand duchess does not slump. We must shine tonight. Shine." She turned to her first maid, the one she'd brought with her from Germany all those many years ago. She spoke quickly in a German dialect. "Honestly, Greet, sometimes I worry she will be mistaken for a peasant."

Greet did not reply to that. She had been long in service to Alexandra, largely due to her ability to not reply. Alexandra liked impertinent servants even less than she liked Jews.

"Is it a party, Mama?" Alexei asked, once the fuss about Anastasia's comportment was done with.

"More than a party," the tsarina said. "A secret as well."

"I love secrets," Alexei said.

"And can keep none of them," Anastasia whispered at him fiercely. Well, she certainly couldn't talk back to her mother. It wasn't allowed. Besides, she'd made the mistake once of telling him something as they played, and he'd scattered it about to the servants and Father Grigori, which meant everyone at the palace soon knew about her crush on Vasili, the portrait painter. Every time Vasili had come into the room, she had blushed the color of sunrise after that, guessing he knew about it, too. She had never forgiven Alexei nor spoken to the portrait painter again.

"Can, too," Alexei said, thinking about all the secrets told to him by Father Grigori he'd never told anyone. And the stories. But he would someday . . . when he was tsar and there were no consequences to what he did and said. Only obedience.

He would know everything about everyone just as his father did. Everything.

Shoring up my co-conspirators had been tougher work than I'd imagined it would be. *Really, they have no stomach for this stuff. Aristocrats are ever prepared to pronounce sentence but rarely willing to carry out that same sentence themselves. Unless it is in a stupid duel. Assassination should be short, brutal, and the outcome without question. Not two men of equal strength and ability flailing about with swords!*

Washing my hands in the large basin as these thoughts banged about in my head, I began to giggle at the over-wrought metaphor.

"I am not Herod," I told the mirror. I forced myself to stop giggling. It wouldn't do to be overheard laughing alone, talking to myself. It would give my wife ammunition to fight any separation.

Then, remembering that Ninotchka was out at some women's gala, and the servants dismissed for the evening, I felt immediately relieved and finished the thought, though quietly, in case the walls were thinner than I believed. "And the mad monk is no Christ!" There! I'd said it aloud.

It was not that I enjoyed getting my hands dirty. *Well, perhaps in this exceptional case. . . .*

"Still, if you really want something done," I said to my image, "occasionally you have to be the one to do it." The image stared back, stern, unyielding. I would have to be certain to carry that face with me to Prince Yusupov's party.

The others wanted the monk dead almost as much as I did. The prince even called him "a meddlesome priest."

But the worry was still with me—could I count on them completely? I shrugged rather dramatically, ran fingers through my hair, then thought: *I have to be certain they do not make me the one to take the blame for Rasputin's death.*

My mind whirled with possibilities. *Other than the poison—and it's enough to fell a bull and its cow besides— their plans are ludicrous. Each has told me privately they will have knives in their boots, revolvers in their waistbands, so that if need be, they can finish the job properly. Stupid aristos. This will only alert him. He has the cunning of a wild creature. He will nose such things out. Besides, once the body is seen by the authorities, it must seem like an ordinary death. The poison is undetectable. Knife wounds and bullet holes scream assassination.*

On the other hand, he thought, *Rasputin himself is the incalculable part of the equation. He has that dark magic on his side. He is a Mesmer. He can make anyone believe that which he tells them to believe.*

I bit my lower lip, thinking the worst of thoughts now:

I cannot presume the others have the will to actually use *their weapons.*

"Better to be prepared myself," I told the mirror. "It will steel my will."

In just a few hours, the mad monk will be dead. I repeated this to myself until I believed it. *And after that—all worries will disappear.*

Hands dried, hair practically as polished as my boots, I found my late father's old dagger that he had never used for anything but opening walnuts. Placing it in the bosom of my shirt, I gave a sudden shudder. I had no pistol.

Everything rested in God's hands now.

An awful thought crept past my wall of confidence: *And the monk has the ear of God.*

"Do not fear," I whispered to myself. "Never fear." It was merely that the sheathed blade was unexpectedly cold against my chest. As if death rested there. Plus, I was now profoundly aware of it.

It is good I am aware of it. I bit my lower lip thoughtfully. *It will remind me to have courage.*

I squared my shoulders and went out into the palace hallway, shutting the door to the apartment behind me with a satisfactory snick.

To my extreme horror and surprise, I saw the misbegotten son of a Siberian peasant marching down the hallway toward me. The mad monk in his best embroidered blouse, black velvet trousers, and shiny new boots.

"Rasputin!" I said under my breath, as if I watched

a dead man walking. *Why is he here? What is he doing? Where is he going?* My thoughts raced as the confidence I had worked so hard to build fled like Russian columns before German infantry. It was too early for the monk to be ready for the evening party. What if he got there too soon and discovered our plans?

"Good evening, Father Grigori," I said as calmly as I could when we drew nearer together, all the while thinking, *What is he doing here? Perhaps he is going somewhere else instead?*

Now I was all but babbling in my head. *Too early or not at all? I don't know which is worse. Could Rasputin dare either? Both? Could he believe he could get away with insulting the prince? Is Rasputin that powerful?*

My hands began to tremble, and I had to will them to stop. Then I subtly put myself into Rasputin's path, so that he would either have to pull up or plow me down.

For a mad moment, I was afraid, thinking he would march right over me. But at the last second, he stopped, looming over me, and I am not a tiny man.

That was when I smelled something odd, a miasma of some sort. It took me a moment to place it. *Cheap soap.* I could barely keep myself from wrinkling my nose. This was no magician, this was a charlatan!

"Out of my way, lackey," Rasputin said, as if the two of us had never been introduced. His eyes were as cold as his mother's breast milk must have been. "I have important news for the tsar."

Now I was truly close to panic. *What news could the monk have to cause him to miss his dinner and insult me openly? Surely he had uncovered our plans!* Surreptitiously, I reached inside my jacket, my fingers touching the hilt of the dagger. It should have given me courage, but all it seemed to do was raise more doubts.

I may have to cut him down here in the hall.

Suddenly I was unsure if I could manage such a thing. *He is far bigger than I am. And if older, certainly stronger.*

I felt sweat pooling under my arms, thought wildly, *If I miss with my first stroke, he could probably snap me in two with his huge peasant's hands.*

"Why not give it to me then, Father," I said, hoping my voice didn't sound as querulous and weak to the monk as it did to me. "I assume by your outfit that you have somewhere else you must be?"

I was really just trying to buy some time. I'd need to be just a few steps back so to have room to draw steel, but not so far away as to be unable to close and strike. But if I did so, I'd no idea what I might tell His Majesty to explain the murder of the tsarina's closest advisor in the halls outside my chambers.

But tales can be fabricated, evidence planted. And though I was not terribly adept with a knife, a man's heart was not a walnut, no matter how shrunken it may be.

Those other skills I had in abundance: manipulation, storytelling, obfuscation.

But the knife would have to come out first.

Before I could pull out the blade, the mad monk spoke in that damnable convincing voice.

"You are right, my son. I have somewhere to be. Somewhere important. The tsar, bless him, is probably already closeted with his beautiful wife. No man should be so disturbed. I will speak to him in the morning after our prayers." He managed to pack information and insult in six short sentences before turning on his heel and marching away.

I watched him disappear around a corner, sweat from my knife hand drip-dripping onto the hilt.

My car followed Rasputin's, but not that closely. I did not want to frighten him off. It soon became clear we were both going to Prince Felix Yusupov's palace.

The prince was sole heir to the largest fortune in Russia, and I was certainly not in his set, so I'd never been inside his house, though I knew where it was. But if I could help pull off this coup, I was certain the prince would reward me greatly.

The prince had once been good friends with the mad monk, pals in carousal, so they say. That was years before he was married. He and Rasputin had gone together to all the dubious night spots. The women they kept company with were dubious as well. But in this marriage, the princess now held the upper hand—her royalty trumped his money. So, Rasputin had been ruled out of the prince's life. An old story but a true one.

But the monk had not taken the hint, so a year ago, Prince Yusupov was heard to complain, "Will no one kill this *starets* for me?"

I hadn't known about it then, but when I spoke of my plan to Pavlovich, he told it to the prince. "A great favor," he was told.

And so things began to boil. But because of Pavlovich's extensive social calendar, the first time he was free was this evening, December 30th. He and I decided that Pavlovich didn't dare cancel any of his previous engagements and thus arouse suspicion.

Suddenly aflame with excitement, I leaned forward. "Faster!" I told the driver. "Faster now."

It was pitch black outside, the true dark of a Russian winter, lit only by the car's lights illuminating swirling snow. The driver had a heavy foot, and soon we approached the prince's palace.

If anything, my mood was even higher than before. I felt that if I got out of the car now, I could dance all the rest of the way there. "Drive around to the servants' entrance," I instructed the driver. "I am a surprise guest."

"Good one, sir!" he answered, making the turn around the back of the palace.

One of the stewards took me down to the cellar room where the dinner was to be held. No one else was there yet.

The cellar room was of gray stone with a granite floor. It had a low, vaulted ceiling and heavy curtains to keep out the cold. I tried peeking out from behind the curtains to get a sense of the room, but I realized immediately that my shoes protruded from underneath. I could not hide there.

The place already felt like a mausoleum. All it needed was a plain coffin. Only the carved wooden chairs, the small tables covered with embroidered cloths, and the cabinet of inlaid ebony indicated that it was a place of habitation. A white bearskin rug and a brilliant fire in the hearth hardly softened the room's cemeterial aspect. Though perhaps knowing the plan for the evening, I exaggerated the sense of finality.

In the very center of the room stood a table that was laid for six: the prince, the monk, Pavlovich, two other conspirators, and the prince's wife, who had been the bait to lure Rasputin to the place. Though the monk was not to know it, Princess Irina was off in the Crimea with her parents, not here.

I smiled, a full, almost boyish grin. *What a plot we have hatched! What a coil.*

A door opened, and I startled, too late to return to the safety of the curtain, but soon realized it was Dr. Lazovert, the purveyor of poisons. He put a finger to his lips, summoning me over.

A samovar in the middle of the table was already smoking away, surrounded by plates of cakes and dainties.

When I got close enough, the doctor pointed to the sideboard where drinks sat.

"Each one filled with poison and the rims of the glasses soaked in poison as well," Dr. Lazovert whispered, adding, "and each cake filled with enough cyanide potassium to kill several men in an instant. It won't matter which he takes up. Just be sure you and the others—and the servants—do not take a taste of anything down here."

I thought, almost gleefully: *Several men! We only want to dispatch one.*

The plan was in motion. I knew what came next. As soon as Rasputin dropped, it was my job to get the body out of there. But just in case the monk was slow to die, I had my knife. And someone else a pistol. Then we'd wrap the body in an old rug the prince had procured and drop it in the Neva, which flowed nearby. The spring floods would take care of the rest.

From upstairs came the sound of music. "Is that 'Yankee Doodle Dandy'?" I asked the doctor. "That damned American song?"

The music was supposed to be part of a party that Princess Irina was throwing for some women friends before joining the men.

The doctor nodded. "Now hide. They will soon be bringing Rasputin down."

Knowing now that the curtain was not a plausible hiding place, I situated myself on the other side of the wooden serving door. It had a small window. I could see, and hear, but not be seen. The main servants were off, having been given a free night and warned not to return 'til morning, with just a few of the most trusted left behind.

"Perfect," I said to the doctor, but he was already heading upstairs.

And then the door from the stairs opened, and down walked the mad monk himself, followed by a nervous-looking Yusupov.

I wanted to shout at the prince, "Stop sweating! You'll give the game away." But we were already well into it. It would play out as it would. I shrank back for a moment, away from the window in the door, took a deep breath, and waited.

Rasputin sauntered into the room, smiling. He could feel his body tingling, starting at his feet. That always meant something huge would happen soon. Perhaps Princess Irina would declare her love openly. Perhaps the prince would simply offer her to him. He had done so before with his other women, when they were both younger and the prince not so caught up in convention. Rasputin made little distinction between a princess and a prostitute in bed. They even liked it better that way.

But no—he preferred the chase, the slow seduction, the whimpering of the whipped dog that would be the prince. He must not jump the fence before it was close enough. His mother always said that. The old folk wisdom was true.

He touched the charm around his neck. The prince would hate him but could not harm him.

"Have some cakes," Prince Yusupov said, gesturing with a hand toward the table. There were beads of sweat on his forehead.

Rasputin wondered at that. It was, indeed, too warm

down in the cellar, but he himself was not sweating. He rarely sweated, except in the baths or in the arms of a beautiful and eager woman.

"The cakes were made especially . . . especially for you," Yusupov said. He hesitated. "To make peace between us."

Rasputin heard the hesitation, thought he understood what that meant. "The cakes will do, Felix," he said. And indeed, they were the very kind he loved best. Honey cakes topped with crushed almonds, *skorospelki* covered with branches of fresh dill, caviar blinis, and so much more. But Rasputin did not want to appear greedy.

"Please," Yusupov said. "Irina had them made especially. We would not want her to be disappointed."

"No, we would not," Rasputin said, managing to make the four words sound both engaging and insulting at the same time. It was not unintentional, and he enjoyed the confused clash of emotions that sparked briefly in Yusupov's eyes. He picked up a honey cake and a blini and ate them, savoring the taste. Surprisingly, they were too sweet and dry. "Some Madeira, if you please," he told the prince.

Yusupov himself went to the sideboard and poured the wine, with exquisite care, into a glass.

The first glass went down quickly but barely moved the dry taste out of Rasputin's mouth. Forgetting that he didn't want to appear greedy, he held out the glass for a refill.

Eagerly, the prince filled it for him.

"And the princess?" Rasputin said, after downing the second glass. His mouth was still dry, but he forswore another glass. He wanted to remember this evening in every crisp detail.

"Here shortly. She had to see off her own guests and then change costume," Yusupov said. "Women!" His voice sounded like a small dog's bark.

"Ah, women," replied the monk. "God bless them. My mother used to say, 'A wife is not a pot, she will not break so easily.' Ha ha. But I would rather say, 'Every seed knows its time.'"

Yusupov started. "What do you mean by that? What do you mean?" He was sweating again.

Rasputin felt a sudden camaraderie with the poor man. *Prince or pauper, young man or old, women make fools of us all.* He put his hand out and clapped Yusupov on the shoulder. "Just that women, God bless them, are like little seeds and know their own time, even though we poor fellows do not." Then he passed a hand across his forehead, and it came away sweaty. "Is it very hot in here?"

"Yes, very," said Yusupov, using a handkerchief to wipe his own forehead.

"Well, sing to me then to pass the time 'til your wife gets here," the monk said, pondering another drink. *Just to fend off this awful heat.* He pointed to the guitar that rested against the wall. "I heard you often singing in those far-off days when we went into the dark sides of the city. I would hear you again. For old times' sake." The camaraderie faded as quickly as it had come, and he leered at the prince. "And for the sake of your lovely wife, Irina."

Yusupov nodded, gulped, nodded again. Then he went over and picked up the guitar. Strumming, he began to sing.

I could not believe my ears. The prince had actually begun singing, slightly off-key.

I moved back and peeked carefully through the window. Rasputin was still on his feet, though there seemed
to be cakes missing from the table. An empty glass stood
on the table as well. And Yusupov, that damned upper-
class clown, was strumming his guitar and singing lustily.
Had he gone faint with worry? It certainly did not sound
so. Had he decided not to kill his old friend after all? I
ground my teeth. It was hard to tell.

I turned away from the sight, raced up the servants'
stairs, and found Dr. Purishkevich and Grand Duke
Dmitri at the top of the stairs that led down to the cellar.

"For the Lord's sake, what is going on?" I asked, my
voice barely more than a whisper. "To my certain knowledge, the monk has eaten several cakes. And had a glass
of wine."

"Two at least," said Dr. Lazovert, joining us on the
stairs. "We heard him ask for a refill. He is. . . ," he whispered as well, "not a man at all, but the very devil. There

was enough poison to fell an entire unit of Cossacks. I know, I put the stuff in it myself." He looked wretched and stank of fear-sweat and rough liquor.

"Pull yourself together," I began, but it was too late. The doctor's eyes had rolled back, and he sank into a stupor.

Purishkevich caught him before he tumbled down the stairs and broke his fool neck. I took his hands to try to revive him.

The grand duke just looked disgusted. At me. "The plan was yours. So what next?"

I finally took it upon myself to slap the doctor's face hard enough that my own hand hurt from the blow. It was more frustration than medicinal, and either way, it did nothing to revive him.

All the while we whispered together, Yusupov's thready voice singing tune after tune made its way up the stairs.

"Should we go down?" I asked, dreading the answer.

"No, no, no," Purishkevich whispered vehemently, "that will give the game away."

"But surely he is already suspicious."

"He is a peasant," said the grand duke, which explained nothing.

I was suddenly a-tremble. After all we had planned— I had planned—for it to come to this? *This is the worst possible outcome.* Oh, had I but known.

Suddenly the door to the cellar opened, and we conspirators all backed up. I have to admit, I was the fastest. But it was just poor Yusupov, saying over his shoulder,

"Have another cake, Father. I will see what is keeping my wife."

And Rasputin's voice, somewhat hoarsened, called up to him, "Love and eggs are best when they are fresh!"

"A peasant," the grand duke repeated, as Yusupov came up to find us.

If the doctor had been trembling, the prince was a leaf on a tree, all aflutter and sweating. "What should I do? What can I do?"

"He cannot be allowed to leave half-dead," Purishkevich said.

The grand duke handed Yusupov a pistol. "Be a man."

At that, Yusupov bent over like an old man from the weight of what he had to do, then went back down the stairs, holding the pistol behind him.

We heard Rasputin call out, "For the Lord's sake, give me more wine." And then he added, "With God in thought, but mankind in the flesh."

A moment later we heard a shot. Though I'd expected it, I still jumped in shock. Then a scream. I didn't think it was Rasputin. Dr. Lazovert sat bolt upright, though I had no idea why a slap and a gunshot couldn't wake him but a scream did.

"Come," said the grand duke, "that will have done it."

Suddenly, I wasn't so sure, but in this company, it was not my place to say.

Two of them ran down the stairs one right after another, the grand duke first, and the quickly recovered

Dr. Lazovert second. Purishkevich stayed behind. And I, trailing a bit later, because I was not actually supposed to be there, came last.

Rasputin had fallen backward onto the white bearskin rug, his eyes closed. There was blood. Much blood.

I felt faint. "Definitely faint," I heard myself saying.

Dr. Lazovert knelt by Rasputin's side, felt for his pulse. He did not seem moved by the blood. In fact, the sight of it seemed to recover him even more.

Perhaps in his profession he is more at ease with blood than poison.

He looked up at us, saying phlegmatically, "He is dead."

But, as it turned out, that was premature. I began to wonder about the doctor's qualifications, for not a moment later, Rasputin's left eye, then his right, opened, and he stared straight at Yusupov with those green eyes that reminded me of dragon eyes. Eyes that were suddenly filled with hate.

The doctor fell back on his rather large behind.

I found myself saying, "I gather that a man arising from sure death is no ordinary occurrence for a doctor." Nobody paid me any attention.

Yusupov screamed. Not like a man, but like some kind of monkey. It had definitely been he who'd screamed earlier, and not Rasputin. Then he began to gibber. *Any second*, I thought, *he will climb the curtains and be away. And I will be right after him.*

But in fact I could not move at all. It was as if we were

all in some sort of horrific fairy tale and had been turned to stone. Neither could poor Yusupov move, though at least he'd stopped screaming.

The grand duke was cursing under his breath. And I thought we were about to lose Dr. Lazovert again, who had struggled to his feet but was looking mighty wobbly, like a man standing in a very high wind.

"Long whiskers cannot take the place of brains," said Rasputin, foam bubbling from his mouth as he spoke. He leaped up, grabbed poor Yusupov by the throat with one hand, and tore an epaulet from the prince's jacket with the other. But Yusupov was sweating so badly, the monk's hand slipped from his throat, and the prince broke away from him, which threw Rasputin down on his knees.

That gave Yusupov time to escape, and he turned and raced up the stairs. He was screaming out to Purishkavich to fire his gun, shouting, "He's alive! Alive!" His voice was inhuman, a terrified scream, more like a strangled cat than a man.

The three of us left in the room watched, frozen with horror and amazement, as Rasputin, down on all fours, foaming and fulminating, climbed the stairs after him.

Prince Yusupov made it to his parents' apartments and locked the door after him, but the mad monk, maddened further by all that had happened to him, went straight out the front door into the frigid night. He no longer had on a coat, and we could only hope he would die soon of both frost and the poisoned drink. Not to mention the gunshot.

The others, equally underdressed for the weather, followed him to see what he would do, Dr. Lazovert muttering all the while that Rasputin was a devil and would probably sprout bat wings and fly away.

But the mad monk neither opened bat wings nor flew. Instead, he careened across the snow-covered courtyard toward the iron gate that led to the street, shouting all the while, "Felix, Felix, I will tell everything to the empress."

At last, Purishkevich raised his gun and fired.

The night seemed one long, dark echo. But he had obviously missed because Rasputin was still standing.

"Fire again!" I cried. "If he gets away and tells his story to the tsar, we are all dead men." Though we had been making so much noise in public now, we were probably dead men anyway.

Purishkevich fired again and, unbelievably, missed once more.

"Fool!" the grand duke said as Purishkevich bit his own left hand to force himself to concentrate.

That there were only a few streetlights made things even more difficult. But as if he were out hunting deer, Purishkevich carefully sighted down the barrel on the running figure. Amazingly, when he fired a third time— his most difficult shot of the evening—it seemed to strike Rasputin between the shoulders. He shuddered, stopped, but did not fall.

"A devil, I tell you," cried the doctor. I could hear his teeth chattering with the cold. Or just with fear. Or both.

"I am surrounded by fools," the grand duke said, and I was inclined to agree with him.

Then Purishkevich shot one last time, and this one hit Rasputin in the head for certain, and he fell to his knees. Purishkevich ran over to him and kicked him hard, a boot to the temple. And with that, the monk finally fell down on his back in the snow.

Suddenly, Yusupov appeared holding a rubber club and began hitting Rasputin hysterically over and over and over again.

The grand duke took hold of the prince's shoulders and led him away. And not unkindly, for someone who had decried him as a fool mere moments ago.

Only then did I take out the knife that was in my shirt and, unsheathing it, walked over to the body and plunged the blade deep into Rasputin's heart. It went into his body so smoothly, I could not believe the ease of it.

I wanted to say something profound, anything—but there was nothing more to say. This time, the mad monk's eyes stayed closed, and he did not arise again.

A servant from the princess's apartment came out a little later with a rope, and they pulled the body over to the frozen Neva and left it there.

"Should we find a hole and push him in?" I asked, eager to be rid of the evidence.

"Let the world see him," the grand duke said. "Dead is dead."

I looked at the mad monk splayed out on the ice and

wondered at that. By my count, Rasputin should have died five times that night before the knife decided the end. But despite my earlier worry about the monk's death being called into question, all I felt then was relief.

"Dead is dead." I agreed and left the body lying there on the river ice.

When I got home, I soaked for an hour in the tub but could not scrub away the feel of my hand touching Rasputin's back, when the knife went deep into his body, as if through fresh butter.

"It is ended," I told my image in the mirror.

But really, it had only begun.

At the Mariinsky Theatre, the tsarina came on stage looking as if she had no idea what was about to happen, but in fact she did. Knowing how much she hated surprises, and how she needed to be prepared, the tsar had told her three days ahead of time about the ceremony. But the rest of the family was not in on the surprise.

The audience was full of noble families. The English and German delegations were there as well. Everyone applauded dutifully—and some even with great excitement—when the tsar made the announcement.

The tsarina put her hand to her breast and looked marvelously surprised, because she had not known her husband was going to make a speech and detail all of the things she had done to earn this medal of honor. And when she stood and made her careful way up the stairs and across the boards towards him, her left hand still rested there on her breast. She looked, one of her friends would tell her later, like a doe crossing the ice, with careful competence and always on alert for possible danger.

Standing by the podium, holding a large bouquet of

flowers, the medal on its ribbon around her neck, she was extremely pleased and still a bit surprised.

Nicholas had spoken about the work she had done to improve conditions for the poorer classes since first coming to Russia as a bride; how she had founded schools and hospitals, never hesitating even when difficult regulations and unbending bureaucrats had tried to stop her. She hadn't known that he had known, which made things all the sweeter and the award—even though she had been warned three days earlier—very surprising. But as her grandmother Victoria probably would have said, "We do it for the glory of God, not the glory of ourselves."

Alexandra raised her arms wide, the flowers in her right hand. She had practiced a speech for three days before the mirror, but in that instant, forgot every word of it. All that came out was: "I love you. I love you, all the Russians. And I thank you for the love that comes back to me as well."

Then there were roars of approval and great cheers. And she thought as she nodded to the audience, who were now on their feet, applauding and calling out her name, "I will remember this moment for the rest of my life."

She turned and mouthed to her husband who was applauding as well, "The rest of my life."

The mad monk lay on the ice. His chest hurt abominably where the knife had plunged in. He couldn't move.

"I curse you," he muttered, or tried to. His lips were frozen shut, and anyway, he wasn't sure whom he should be cursing, not knowing who had set the blade deep in his chest. Instead, he cursed his old drinking companion, his betrayer.

Felix, may your world crumble.

A dead man's curse is a powerful thing, and he knew that the Lord listened at that moment.

May every living thing you touch wither and die.

He could feel his curse take hold and bend the very fabric of the world.

And may you lose everything you hold dear.

The cursing done, he continued to take stock of his wounds.

His shoulder and the back of his head hurt, too, though not as badly as the hole in his heart. Oddly enough, his stomach and throat were burning as well. He wondered if the cakes—how many had he eaten?—had disagreed with him. *Trust the courtiers to make stale and rotten cakes. His own mother could have done better.*

And though he judged several of the wounds mortal, they did not worry him. He was wearing his charm, so men couldn't kill him. Nor women, it turned out. The whore who long ago had slit him from stem to sternum had learned that. He would survive the wounds.

But the cold?

The Russian cold was not just death for a man. It was death for armies. For nations.

But it is not death for God, nor his chosen messenger!

He was cold, he decided, but he had been colder. The Lord knew how cold a *moujik* from Siberia could get without succumbing. And though these thoughts cheered him, they didn't change the fact that he could not move. Moving warmed the blood. Moving warmed the soul. There was no life without movement. And it wasn't just for himself that he worried.

How long 'til the full moon? he thought. *How long 'til that fool Lenin arrives and lets the dragons out of their holes?*

Dragons, when caught in their lairs, can be drowned, starved out, slaughtered by massed rifle fire—in fact, killed in any number of ways. It was why the tsar's dragons' stables were better guarded than his own home. In the skies, they were unstoppable: swift fire from on high and death to all who stood against them, like Jews and revolutionaries. But not now.

The fools haven't killed me. But if I don't recover before the moon is full, they will have killed Russia.

He tried to twitch a finger, blink an eyelid. Nothing.

I must rest. I will try again in the morning.

The moon rose over the frozen Neva, a near perfect circle.

I have perhaps two days, he thought, his body cold but his mind perfectly clear. *Maybe three.*

The red dragons were no longer restless because, for the first time, they'd been led up into the night air. Long noses sniffed at the sky; wings unfurled and caught the slight breeze. But they were not loosed to fly. Not yet. Not 'til Lenin gave the word.

The man in question, who had arrived just the night before, stood watching the dragons. His eyes were closed almost to slits, as if he stood in full armor, assessing the troops through the slot in his visor.

Bronstein knew the Bolshevik leader had never seen dragons before tonight, but he was showing neither awe nor fear in their presence. On the contrary, he was eyeing them critically, one hand stroking his beard. Somehow, that unnatural calm made the man seem even more dangerous.

At last he turned to Bronstein, the eyes no longer in slits, just a bit tired, with bags under them as if he didn't get much sleep. "You are sure they will function, Leon?"

Lenin meant him, Bronstein. He insisted on calling Bronstein by his revolutionary name. Bronstein realized just now that he didn't much care for it. It was an ugly name, *Leon. And Trotsky sounds like a town in Poland.* He wondered how soon he could go back to the name he'd been born with. And he thought at the same time that taking revolutionary names was like a boy's game. *Such silliness.*

"Leon!" Lenin snapped. "Will they function?"

"I . . . I do not know for sure," Bronstein said too quickly, knowing he should have lied and said he was certain. Knowing that he had little capacity to say something was true if it was not. "But they are the same stock as the tsar's dragons," he added. "And those function well enough."

Bronstein was certain of that, at least. He'd traced the rumor of a second brood bred from the Great Khan's dragons with the thoroughness of a Talmudic scholar. Traced the rumor through ancient documents detailing complex treaties and byzantine trades to a kingdom in North Africa. Traced it by rail and camel and foot to a city that drought had turned to desert when the pharaohs were still young. Traced it with maps and bribes and a little bit of luck to a patch of sand that hadn't seen a drop of rain in centuries.

Then he'd dug.

And dug.

And dug some more.

He dug 'til he'd worn through three shovels and done what he was sure was irreparable damage to his arms and shoulders. Dug 'til the sun scorched the Russian pall from his face and turned it to dragon leather. Dug 'til the desert night froze him colder than any Russian would ever care to admit.

Dug 'til he found the first new dragon eggs in more than a hundred twenty years. The tsar's dragon queen hadn't dropped a hatch of eggs in a century, nor was she likely to anytime soon. And even if she did, it would be years before the eggs brought forth young.

Dragon eggs weren't like other eggs. They didn't need warmth and heat to produce hatchlings. They were already creatures of fire; they needed a cool, damp place to develop.

Nothing colder and wetter than a Russian spring, Bronstein knew. So he brought them home in giant wooden boxes and planted them on the hillside overlooking his town, doing all the work himself.

And another thing that set dragon eggs apart: they could sit for years, even centuries, until the conditions were right to be born.

"And some would say," Bronstein said to Lenin, "they should be more powerful having lain in their eggs for so much longer."

Lenin stared at him blankly for a moment, then turned to Koba. "Are your men ready?"

Koba grinned, and his straight teeth reflected orange from the fire of a snorting dragon. The handler calmed the beast as Koba spoke.

"Ready to kill at my command, Comrade."

152

Lenin turned a stern gaze to the moon, as if he could command it to rise faster. Koba glanced at Bronstein and grinned wider.

A dragon coughed a gout of flame, and Koba's eyes reflected the fire. Bronstein looked into those eyes of flame and knew that if Lenin let Koba loose the men before he—Bronstein—launched his dragons, then he had lost. There would be no place for him in that new Russia. The land would be ruled by Georgian murderers and cutthroat thieves—new *kruks* to replace the old, and the proletariat worse off than before. Not the Eden he'd dreamed of. And the Jews? Well, they, of course, would be blamed.

"Lenin," Bronstein said, as firmly as he could. "The dragons are ready."

"Truly?" Lenin asked, not looking back.

"Yes, Comrade."

Lenin waited just a beat, nothing more, then said, "Then let them fly."

Bronstein nodded to Lenin's back and practically leapt toward the dragons. "Fly!" he shouted. "Let them fly!"

The command was repeated down the line. Talon-boys dashed bravely beneath broad, scaly chests to cut the webbings that held the dragons' claws together.

"Fly!" Bronstein shouted, and the handlers let slip the rings that held the pronged collars tight to the dragons' necks, before scurrying back, as the beasts were now free to gnash and nip with teeth the size of scythe blades.

"Fly!" the lashers shouted as they cracked their long whips over the dragons' heads. But the dragons needed no encouragement. They were made for this. For the night sky, the cool air, the fire from above.

"Fly," Bronstein said softly as giant wings enveloped the moon, and the Red Terror took to the skies.

The last of the beasts to take flight was the first hatched and the largest, the leader of the brood. Dragons, like modern man it seemed, led from the rear. As the beast stood poised on an outcropping, wings outspread and testing the night air, it craned its long neck back to look directly at Bronstein, who felt a wave of heat and fury wash over him, through him. The heat was the dragon's, but he recognized the fury as his own. He wanted to burn the country as badly as the dragons did. He wanted to punish them for Siberia. For his people. For himself.

The dragon bared its teeth in a reptilian smile and leapt into the air.

Bronstein suddenly knew that he had indeed spent too long a time with the dragons. *I have become them. Their rage. Their fire.*

He looked over to Lenin and saw hot fury in his slitted eyes as well.

But he has spent so little time with them. . . . Another thought, more profound, pushed that one away: *Some men are born dragons, and some become them.*

And the rest flee or are burnt to ash.

He watched in horror as Lenin turned to Koba. "Release your men to do their duty, as well." And Koba laughed in answer, waving his hand.

Bronstein saw Koba's men scurry away and knew for certain that Russia was lost. Releasing the dragons was a mistake; releasing Koba's men was a disaster. Borutsch had been right all along.

It will be years before we struggle out of these twin terrors from land and sky. What I wanted was a clean start. But this is not it. He shivered in the cold.

I need warmth, he realized suddenly. By that he did not mean a stove in a tunnel, a cup of tea, schnapps. *I want palm trees. Soft music. Women with smiling faces. I want to live a long and merry life, with a zaftik wife.* He thought of Greece, southern Italy, Mexico. *For if the Russian winter cannot quell the hot fury in me, perhaps some southern heat can mask it.*

The dragon wings were but a murmur now. And the shouts of men.

In the blackness before dawn, the mad monk's left index finger moved. It scraped across the ice, and the slight *scritching* sound it made echoed loud and triumphant in his ears.

He'd lain unmoving for three days.

A peasant child had thrown rocks at him on the second day, trying to ascertain whether the drunk on the ice was alive or dead. The mad monk was surprised when the child didn't come out on the ice and loot his body. But then he realized why.

The ice was melting.

The days had grown warmer, and the ice was melting. Soon, the mighty Neva would break winter's grip and flow freely to the Baltic Sea once more. Icy water was already pooling in his best boots and soaking his black velvet trousers. It splashed in his left ear, the one that lay against the ice, and he thought he could feel it seeping through his skin to freeze his very bones.

Terror crept in with the cold as he realized that his attempted murderers would not need to kill him. The river would do their work for them. Drown him as his sister had drowned, or waste him away in fever like his brother. He would have shivered with fear or cold, but he could not move.

Night fell, and for the first time, Father Grigori felt the terror of the mortals he'd ministered to. Through the night, he felt like Jesus on the cross, his iron faith wavering. *Why hast thou forsaken me?*

The night brought no answer, just more cold water in his boots. More icy water in his beard. More cold seeping into his bones.

But then, before dawn, the finger.

If one finger can move, the rest can as well.

And putting thought to deed, he moved the index finger on his other hand. Moved it as if he'd never been hurt, tapping it on the ice, once, twice, a third time. His spirits soared as the sun broke the horizon, and with a great effort, he bent up at the waist, levering himself to a sitting position. He was sore. He was cold. Every bit of his body ached. But he was alive. And moving!

However, he was also very tired, and he decided not to try to stand quite yet. Facing the rising sun, he waited for the heat to reach him.

"When I am warmed straight through," he said, his voice calm despite the creaking and popping of his stiff limbs, "I shall go ashore and deal with Felix and the others."

Watching the sun rise and turn from red to gold, he saw a flock of birds pass before it. A big flock of birds, not just in size, but in number, hundreds of them, casting long shadows across the ice.

What are those? he thought. *Egrets leaving their roost?* But it was winter. There were no egrets here.

And the birds were too big.

Even from far away, he could tell they were huge. Larger even than the Siberian golden eagles he had hunted with in his youth.

Suddenly, he knew he was too late. He'd lain on the ice too long. And Lenin had come to loose the Red Terror on the land.

Now staring in horror, he watched the flock move closer, revealing red scales and leathery wings, smoke curling from their nostrils.

He made a small cry, like a rabbit in extremis, and struggled to stand. But the movement that had come so easily just moments before was a trial now. His limbs cried in protest and refused to budge. Despite straining and sweating, he'd only achieved an ungainly half-crouch when the dragons were upon him.

The lead dragon swooped in low and swatted him aside with its forefoot. He went skittering across the ice, feeling his ribs shatter. Crawling for the shore, his fingernails broke on the ice as he dragged himself along far too slowly.

Finally—*finally*—he was able to shiver. But this was in fear. He no longer felt cold. Terror rushed hot in his blood.

A shadow enveloped him, and he looked up into the black eyes of a hovering dragon. Before he could react, the dragon's talons shot toward him, and one long claw pierced him through the chest, pinning him to the ice. It looked as if it were laughing at him, its teeth filling its horrible great mouth. He tried to scream, but suddenly he had no breath. Lungs pierced, he could only stare stupidly as the dragon's wingbeats slowed and it landed on the ice beside him, as gently as any songbird.

But the dragon was no songbird, and the ice shattered under its weight. Water splashed the beast's belly, and it roared its displeasure, flapping madly trying to get aloft. Then it belched out a lash of fire, which further melted the ice around itself and the ice below Rasputin.

When the dragon managed to lift out of the water, it slowly shook itself free of water and prey at the same time. The wind from the dragon's wings was so strong, it pushed Father Grigori Rasputin over the melting edge of ice and down into the dark water.

We have put a rope through the nose of Leviathan, he thought as the waves closed over his head. He could still see the dragons, distorted by the water, hovering over the hole in the ice like terns. *But he is king over all the sons of pride.*

And then like his sister, Maria, so many years before, his throat and lungs filling so swiftly with the cold water that he could not even cough, Father Grigori Rasputin drowned.

When the tsarina was told about Rasputin, it was her husband who broke the news.

He took her on his knee, as he had when the children were still young and asleep in the nursery, watched over by three different babushkas. "Old women never sleep well at night, so they will stay awake," he had told her, as he had been told by one of his cousins when the first child was born.

He held her tenderly in his arms and whispered to her, as if a prelude to their lovemaking. "Sunny, my darling girl, I have news I can barely make my lips speak."

She turned to him, eyes wide with fear. "Alexei. . . ."

He shook his head. "Sleeping soundly. No, not about him."

She named each of the children in order except—of course—their dead daughter, already out of the reach of such terror.

She stood. "Tell me standing. I am Victoria's grand-daughter; I am the child of Germans who was taught in the cradle to handle any bad news."

He stood, holding her at arms' length. "It is Father Grigori," he said.

She shook her head. "No! No! He is not old. He has not been sick. He is on speaking terms with God."

He looked down at the floor, before gathering the courage to look once again in her eyes. "He was murdered," he said. "Foully murdered." He couldn't stop himself now, and the words came out in a flood. "Shot, stabbed, poisoned, drowned."

She stared at him as if she had lost all reason. As if the world as she knew it had suddenly collapsed at the center. He wondered if she would look like that when he died.

Then suddenly, she said in a voice as fierce as Baba Yaga's, "Which *thing* killed him?" As if she would bring the miscreant gun or knife or bottle of poison—or river—to trial for the deed.

"All of them," he said, sounding as miserable as if he had been the one to raise a hand to the monk.

She nodded. "It would have needed them all to tear him from the side of the Romanovs," she said.

He took her back into the cavern of his arms but didn't mention the dragons. He didn't dare.

She slept all night in his arms, something she hadn't done in years, so there was one thing he could bless Rasputin for.

At the dawning of the day, the tsarina went into the children's rooms to tell them about what had happened before the news leaked from unreliable sources, such as servants, into their innocent ears. When she returned from that awful task, the tsar was already in his own bedroom, where he was sequestered with his barber. She was not even out of her nightclothes, and her own hair seemed to have grown gray in places overnight.

"You bastard!" she shouted, but in German so the barber would not know what she had said. "It was your own bloody dragons in the end."

He took a towel from the barber and wiped his face clean of the shaving soap. "The end of what?"

Luckily, she knew him for the guileless fool he often was, and her anger was becalmed, a ship in troubled waters still, but the sails not flapping dangerously.

She sat down on the nearest chair. "My saintly Father Grigori," she said, her voice dangerously low and careful, "survived everything those bastards used on him." She was still speaking in German, being careful that the barber did not understand what was being said. "And he had already made his escape, 'til the dragons came and drowned him in the Neva."

"That cannot be," the tsar remarked, way too casually to be believed. In fact, he had his answers well prepared. "The dragons are never released without my permission." He tried to smile, feared it was a grimace. "You and I were at the theater. . . ."

"Nevertheless, that is what everyone is saying," she responded. Everyone being the servants, of course.

He was too upset to continue in German and roared out in Russian, "Who is everyone?"

She flapped her hands, too stunned to speak, for he had never before raised his voice with her. She turned and pointed to her rooms, where he could hear her women gossiping.

When he turned to speak to the barber, to calm things down, the man had already fled.

There'll be no help from that quarter, he thought and looked back to his wife. She looked at him as cold as a St. Petersburg winter.

In the time it took for Nicky to turn to the fleeing barber and back again, the tsarina remembered who and what she was.

A German and a queen.

"You made me turn Father Grigori away," she said, coldly. In Russian now, so he couldn't misunderstand her, easily forgetting the truth of the matter. "I turned him away, and now he is dead." Her newly restored strength faltered. "He is dead, and now who will look after little Alexei?" She knew in her heart that the doctors were useless. Only God and Father Grigori had ever been truly helpful to her son.

And now if he takes a turn for the worse? As he will, she thought wildly, *as he always did*. She shuddered to think of it, for there would be no one to help then. *No one but God.*

And then she knew what she had to say, had to insist upon. Her son needed it. Her kingdom required it. History demanded it.

"You will destroy them," she said. She softened her voice, because soft words rather than shouted demands were the most effective tool with her husband. "Please, Nicky, you must."

Nicky looked confused. "Who?" he asked, no longer shouting.

The tsarina knew that the Lord was a loving God, but a vengeful one, too. And if a servant of his had been killed—*murdered!*—then should not they be murdered in return?

We will make this sacrifice to the Lord our God, and Alexei will be spared.

She knew it was right and true and was shocked that Nicky could not see it as clearly. But she also knew how to handle him to get her way.

"The dragons, of course. They killed the only man— the holy man—who might have healed our baby boy."

He stared at her for a long moment before saying, "I give you everything, my darling. My heart, my kingdom, our children. You lack for nothing. Please, please do not ask for this."

"I am not asking. A tsarina does not beg," she said. There were no tears in her eyes.

"When it is necessary," he said, in a voice equally steely, one she almost didn't recognize as his, "a tsar will. I ask, no I *beg* you to consider this: the dragons are our only protection. The family's own protection."

"They bring death to both the unholy and the holy," she told him, her voice low, controlled. "They are indiscriminate. They will kill us if they can."

"Never," he said, but the shudder in his voice gave him away.

The tsar would hear none of it, but the tsarina was relentless. Sometimes raging, sometimes coldly quiet. I watched her worry him like a terrier with a rat for days.

She was not subtle. She spoke about it in public so even functionaries like me heard her anger, her pain. I knew it was a foregone conclusion from the start. He may have been the most powerful man in Russia, but like most men, he was powerless against her. He was like an ordinary man being blown about in the wind.

And she was the wind.

It went on for a week, and the entire court watched it happen, whispered about it, wondered. I could all but hear them think: "Well, she is a German, and you know how they are."

But I, who was faceless and nameless to so many of them, understood what they did not. This had nothing to do with her being German. It had more to do with him being a man too caught up in love. Never a good idea for an ordinary man. Worse for a prince. Disaster for a tsar. I blame his parents for letting him become weak.

So it was no surprise when he sent for me to gather the dragon boys and meet him and a small contingent of soldiers down in the pens.

He made a hash of it, of course, sending the soldiers in first to shoot the beasts, then changing his mind before they could raise their rifles.

By that point, the dragons were suspicious—they are not foolish creatures. And when the dragon boys went in with their sharp knives to dispatch their charges humanely, they were met with claws and teeth and no small amount of flame. The soldiers had to open fire to save the boys, which, as you might imagine, had mostly the opposite effect.

The barns ran black with dragons' blood. A dozen dragon boys died in the slaughter.

Standing at the half-closed door to the barns, I escaped the worst of it, but even I was blooded. Even now, my face bears scars from those hot flames. Though I tell people now I got the scars in the war. And in a way, I suppose, I did.

Few dragons died easily. None died silently. The palace walls rang out with their death cries.

The remaining dragon boys wept for both their brethren and their dragons.

The tsarina seemed jubilant and claimed that God had been appeased and her children were safe.

I knew differently. For as the tsar slaughtered his best weapons of war, a messenger came to the palace and passed me a note.

A rebellion had begun. And the rebels had brought their own dragons.

I didn't pass the message along. There was no time.

I ran to my apartments but did not wake Ninotchka.

All is falling apart, I thought. *She will need her sleep.*

Prying open the old desk where I kept my treasures, I filled my pockets with gold coinage, my real certificate of birth, my other papers, several strands of rare pearls, my mother's diamonds, my father's gold watch and fob. Small reward for the time I had given to tsar and country, but it would have to serve. I left Ninotchka what paltry jewels she had. I had bought them for her, and I knew how little they were worth.

She will need them, I thought. *Alas, the tsar will not look kindly on me and mine once the full story of the mad monk's death comes out. And come out it will. The prince and those other fools will have boasted in private. It's in the blood. Servants can be forced to tell what their masters will not.* I sighed. *Better to leave Ninotchka to what fate her beauty can buy her.*

Most importantly, I grabbed the stolen plans for the drachometer. Those, more than any money or jewels, would buy me a place in the new order of things.

I planned to cross the lines, find the men who held the new reins of terror. Without dragons, the tsar cannot win. History shows us that. And only a fool fights to the very last in a forlorn hope.

I am no fool. I am a man of action, not inaction. I read history. Every wheel turns and turns again. Revolution is a messy business. But history demands the surefooted.

I said aloud—but not too loud, for I only needed to confirm it for myself before I took the giant step into the unknowns of revolt and revolution—"There is always a need for a good functionary, a secretary, a man of purpose."

I thought: *If necessary, I can kill. My hand can wield a knife. I have done it once, can do it again.* My plan had succeeded, even before the dragon coup d'etat.

Yes, I am someone who has much to offer, to moujik or tsar. And I will let it be known—I work equally well with men and with dragons.

It took only a few weeks for Russia to fall. The red dragons saw to that. They didn't terrorize the countryside, but the palaces and houses of the aristocrats. Many of the aristos fled the country with no more than the jewels on their backs. Some had houses elsewhere—in Europe if they were lucky. They carried their titles with them to be sold when they could. But most, the ones who were property-poor, ended up with nothing.

It took much longer for the tsar to admit defeat, but on the 15th of March, he finally abdicated his throne. For the safety of his family, he agreed to the rebel terms. He knew that he was now only citizen Nicholas Romanov and practiced that name in front of any bit of mirror he could find. If there was gall in the breath it took to say it, he did it for the children's sake, and his wife's. *Not*, he thought, *my own*.

But all the while, he tried to send messages to their many cousins ruling in the safe kingdoms of Europe and the United Kingdom.

He got no answers in return.

That silence is as sharp as the spear in our Savior's side, he thought but kept it to himself. And the bitterness compounded when Sunny scolded him for not letting them leave weeks earlier for Germany.

Soon, Citizen Romanov and his family were moved out to Tsarskoye Selo and placed in protective custody by the provisional government at Alexander Palace. Again he stayed silent for the family's sake. Making what few bargains he could for better food, or an easier place for the children and Alexandra to sleep. For himself, he found it no longer mattered.

They stayed but a short time at Alexander Palace, and then—after a long and unpleasant boat trip—wound up in a dismal place called Tobolsk in Siberia, a town of twelve thousand peasants. Two thousand miles from Petrograd. More miles from the capital. From the society of their friends. From civilization.

I do not miss civilization, the tsar told himself, *or at least not nearly as much as I thought.*

"*Maman,*" the girls whispered to her in French, sure that none of their guards could understand it. "We are under guard, underfed. . . ." And Anastasia added, "underappreciated." It was not meant as a joke, but still the girls giggled.

The tsarina (ex-tsarina, she reminded herself, Citizen Alexandra Romanov, a name she was coming to loathe) worried less about the girls and more about Alexei.

The trip had been extremely hard on him, especially as it began on his thirteenth birthday. By the end of the first day's excitement—because the actual reasons for the trip were being kept from the rest of the family—Alexei was exhausted. And exhaustion was never his friend.

The girls had, early on, figured out something was not right, because there were few amenities on the boat, and the boatmen—unlike those on the royal yacht—were rough and grizzled and, frankly, mean.

But it was Alexandra who bore the brunt of the worries, especially as it was likely there would be no competent physicians out there in the back of beyond to heal Alexei.

She worried: *What if he should start bleeding again? What if he falls down and breaks a bone . . . or hits his head and there is a bleed in his brain? He is such an active child. If only he were a quieter, more serious boy. But, though small for his age, and knowledgeable about his illness, he always wanted to be as boisterous as other boys.* Her head spun with fears, and with the knowledge that nothing was now under her control, and that surely God had abandoned her.

The one blessing was that Alexei seemed to be taking

the trip as an adventure. None of the rest of them had the heart to tell him otherwise.

She could tell the girls understood the dangers. They held back tears in public, but with her below deck, they were weepy and inconsolable.

Citizen Alexandra kept reminding herself of her German ancestors, which helped her stay—at least outwardly—steady, calm, and strong. But it was a struggle.

On the second day of the journey, the boat of exile passed by Pokrovskoye, the birthplace of the much-mourned Father Grigori. One of the other ladies pointed out his house, and it was exactly as he had often described it, and easy to identify among the *izbas*.

She was holding her son's hand when they sailed past the house, and she suddenly remembered something Rasputin had said to her, several months before he was murdered. They had been speaking of illness in general, and death in particular. And he had stared at her with those mesmerizing eyes. She thought at that moment that his eyes were like whirling planets. Indeed, he had looked quite, quite mad. She'd realized then that he was no longer there with her, but somewhere else, somewhere in time, in space.

Oh, his body had been standing before her, but he was not there really. In a voice both like and unlike his own, he spoke in a harsh whisper. "Tsarina, to be clear—*my* death will be *your* death."

And then suddenly, the prophet had disappeared, and dear Father Grigori was back. His eyes normal. He had even winked at her, which was the oddest thing of all.

Remembering this, her fingers tightened around her son's hand so hard that Alexei cried out. When they both looked down, bruises—already the size and shape of her fingers—were brightening on his hand.

"Oh, my little tsarevitch," she said, dropping to her knees and kissing each bruise as if she could kiss them away.

"It is nothing, Mama," he said in a voice that was already starting to roughen, like a man's.

They had a few months of relative quiet in Tobolsk, a time that seemed endless to them all. Once they settled in, the bourgeois people of the town treated them as if they were still great folks, not plain Nicholas Romanov and his desperate family. Not "German Alix," as the tsarina had so often been called, and her unmarried daughters. Not "that poor boy who will never be tsar." They tipped their hats to the tsar and Alexei, waved handkerchiefs at the girls and the tsarina. They brought the family and their few servants fresh fruit and vegetables in season.

If the family thought this was to be their long-term

fate, they resigned themselves to it with a certain grace. But the government decided to punish them further by taking away milk, butter, sugar, coffee, and cream. In another country, that might not have seemed much punishment. To Russian aristos, it felt like doom.

And then in April, a man called Jakolav came to the town, and the girls immediately giggled, and one of them called him a "jackal." He did not understand the English and so took no offense.

His visage was like a demon's, a long nose, and hair that never flattened down around his ears, leading the tsar to whisper to his wife: "Perhaps they are pointed!"

She responded in her own whisper, "Perhaps he is Koschei the Deathless," meaning that character from Russian folklore that had so frightened the girls when they were little, whenever he appeared in puppet plays and ballets and stories, though Alexei—even as a sick child—seemed to enjoy it all.

But the demon, the jackal, brought them nothing to enjoy. He had basically come with their death warrants. He wanted Citizen Romanov to come with him, to leave without the family. What little protection they had was being stripped from them.

Nicholas stood, trembling with rage. "I will not go anywhere," he said, his voice hoarse with courage.

Alexandra rose from her own chair and made her way over to him, placing her hand in his.

Jakolav protested: "I beg of you not to refuse. If you do not go with me, they will send a less scrupulous sort of man to take my position."

Anastasia said to her sisters, again in English, "Sending a lion to take the jackal's place!" But this time, none of them laughed. They suddenly understood the seriousness of their situation.

The jackal added, "If you do not want to go alone, you could take with you the people you desire. Be ready; we are leaving tomorrow at four o'clock."

He clicked his heels and left, and no sooner had the door closed than the tsarina began pacing between the tsar and the chair, muttering, "Oh, God! What a ghastly torture! This is the first time in my life that I am not sure what I should do."

The tsar was stunned. He'd never seen her in this state. It all but unmanned him, as if he'd only had strength borrowed from her all these years.

Then he snapped, "You need to do nothing, it is I—"

And that seemed to decide her. "'I will not let you go alone. That man, that jackal," and she smiled bravely at the girls who giggled back, "did you see that nose, that hair? He is not to be trusted." Then she added, "We are a family. I will go with you. The children will follow after."

He did not contradict her.

The details of how they all got to where they ended up matter little. But where they ended up was in a small, barricaded house.

None of them could see the sky from inside the house. The barricades reached the second floor, the windows were all painted shut. No one could look in. No one could look out.

Anastasia, the most daring of the girls, was driven to despair by the lack of a horizon and managed once to open a window to look out. A shot rang out, hit somewhere close. She saw that the bullet lodged in the woodwork of the window frame and slammed the window back down. She was shaken by the shot, so near, but understood then that the sharpshooter had wanted it there in the frame, not in her heart. He could have just as easily killed her on the spot.

None of them even walked by a window after that.

They were searched almost daily, a hard thing for the tsar and tsarina to endure, but the girls were even more mortified by being touched by the guards who were the same ones who leered at them as they walked to and from the single toilet. In fact, the guards wrote scurrilous messages and ribald verses on the walls of the toilet.

The girls—princesses no longer—learned to cloud their eyes as they walked by, heads still held high.

Perhaps worst of all, the family was allowed but five minutes a day to walk in the garden, breathe the air, see the sky.

Sometimes, if Alexei was doing poorly, the tsar would carry him out in his arms or on his back, almost as if he didn't want the child's feet to touch the bitter earth.

The tsarina rarely left the porch. She complained of aches and pains. Each day, the girls found even more gray hairs in her once luxurious crowning glory.

One Sunday, they were allowed to go to Mass. Alexei looked around at the saints' faces in the icons. It was a small, poor church so there were only a few treasures. The girls sat shivering, four of them in the pew, not from the cold—it was the middle of July—just that something seemed ominous about the whole thing. The tsar sat forward, his elbows on the next pew, his head in his hands. The tsarina sat bolt upright, like a warrior or a martyr, hands together. But if she was praying, no sound came from her closed lips.

The following Tuesday, they were let out into the garden for their usual five minutes.

There was a kind of buzz in the air, too loud for bees, too quiet for thunder.

The tsarina looked up, hoping, praying that planes were coming to rescue them. She whispered to herself, *Maybe my German cousins are at the controls.*

For the first time in weeks, she moved out into the garden to see.

Not planes, but birds. Giant birds.

Then she shook her head: *not birds.*

Looking at the tsar, who was playing with Alexei, at the girls pulling small flowers from the ground to wind in their hair, she whispered in a desperate voice, hope and fear entwined: "Nicky, beloved. It's your dragons! Your dragons! Coming to rescue us."

She thought wildly, even happily, *He must not have killed them as I demanded. God stayed his hand and let them live. And now they repay us with release!*

The buzz of the giant beasts came closer.

The guards were screaming, howling. Some fired into the air, but either the dragons were too fast for them or their skin too tough.

The tsarina began to dance like a madwoman.

The tsar, still holding his son, came close. "No my darling, Sunny. My black dragons are all dead. I watched them die. I stood boot-deep in their blood. Those are red dragons. Red. Not mine."

"Red dragons?" As she said it, she remembered how Father Grigori had died. How the revolutionaries had won. Remembered the priest's ghost saying, "My death will be your death."

She understood now. He did not mean it as a metaphor. It was true.

She looked again at the sky, into the death that Father Grigori had prophesied, a fire she did not fear. God had not abandoned her. He had sent a different kind of release. It would be a quick dying for all of them, not this slow descent into madness. Into dirt.

"Fire cleanses. Releases," she told them. "Welcome it. It will make martyrs of us all."

They turned as one and stared at her—her husband, her daughters, and little Alexei as well. Their faces wore masks of fear, horror.

Anastasia screamed.

But Alexandra showed them what they all should do, what a ruler needed to do to win the hearts of the people. She stood tall, threw her arms wide open, and welcomed the heat of paradise into her grieving heart.

And the tsar first, then the girls, and Alexei at the last followed her lead into that furnace and were cleansed.

AH, DON'T LOOK SO SURPRISED, and stop gawping up at me like a fresh-caught fish. Were you not listening? Did I not tell you exactly what I was capable of? Did you think this story ended any other way than with you bleeding out before me?

It's not your fault, of course. Tough, though, that you are the one who pays for it. And isn't that always the way of it? You trusted too much the story of my innocent incompetence and not enough the parts about my ruthlessness.

Your superiors are the ones who should have known better than to send a boy to guard a wily old fox like me. They thought there was nowhere left for me to run. They couldn't have been more wrong. I'll go to the Americans. Or the Germans. None of them like the Communists. I'm certain they'll forgive my relatively minor crimes for the things I know.

Though I doubt I'll tell them the whole truth.

I saved that for you poor, dying soldier boy.

So in your last moments, take solace in the fact that you are one of the very few who know the truth. The absolute truth.

About me.

About the revolution.

And certainly about the dragons.

A SNARKY NOTE ABOUT DRAGONS AND HISTORY

This is a work of fantasy fiction surrounded with—and drowned in—history. Much of it is true.

Not the dragons, of course, but then you already knew that. Or else you took it for a metaphor for the Red Russians, as opposed to the White Russians, many of whom were prescient enough to have already headed for America and elsewhere. If that all sounds kind of Wonderlandish—well, so does the whole Russian Revolution.

A couple of the characters are made up, but not the tsar's family, Leon Trotsky, or Rasputin or his death. (Except for the dragons, of course.)

Adam and his old band—Boiled in Lead—used to play a rousing version of the European pop disco Boney M's "Rah, Rah Rasputin." And Jane minored in Russian Literature and Religion at Smith College. Plus Jane's grandparents on both sides were from Russian "states"—

Ukraine and Latvia. So in some ways, this was a story bound to happen.

The only main character we made up is the nameless functionary, the bureaucrat. And if you are sharp-eyed, you will have noticed that he is the only character in first person. And possibly the author of this novella. That's because when all the leaders die, the functionaries, the bureaucrats, go on. Without them, things—well—stop functioning. They are the ones who decide what to keep and what to burn in the histories. Or they write the histories, much of which is made up. It's our small joke.

The brutal deaths of the entire Romanov family were not of course cleanly and quickly done by dragons. They were shot, bayoneted, and finally, one of the girls trying to crawl away was bludgeoned. The Russians were nothing if not thorough. Then the tsar and his family were buried in secret while the newly formed government spent years insisting the Romanovs were merely in exile. Repeat as often as necessary: there were no actual dragons.

We had written a bunch of short stories together before writing "The Last Tsar's Dragon." Those stories were published in a variety of anthologies. We'd also written a young adult graphic novel trilogy, and four or five middle grade novels, so we had our mother-son partnership down pat. No real arguments but a lot of "forceful conversations" along the way.

Then an invitation to a dragon anthology came to Jane in the mail. She thought she was done writing dragon stories. There was her *There Be Dragons* collection; the young adult *Pit Dragon Chronicles* (in four volumes); an Arthurian middle grade novel, *The Dragon's Boy*; a graphic novel, *The Last Dragon*; lots of dragon poems; and a few dragon picture books. In fact, she was about to say no to the anthology, when two lines popped into her head. "The dragons were harrowing the provinces again. They did that whenever the tsar was upset with the Jews."

Now Jane had already published two novels about the Holocaust (*The Devil's Arithmetic* and *Briar Rose*) and was about to start on a third (*Mapping the Bones*). Plus she'd written a book of poems about her father's family's immigration in the early 1900s from Ukraine because the tsar's dragons—the Cossacks—had indeed been harrowing the Jews (*Ekaterinoslav*). So Jane guessed there was maybe one last dragon story in her. But not to write alone.

She sent Adam the two lines that she had thought of and told him about the anthology invitation, saying: "Want to play?" And the dragon game was afoot.

That story was finished in about four months and accepted and printed in *The Dragon Book: Magical Tales from the Masters of Modern Fantasy*, edited by Jack Dann and Gardner Dozois, Ace, 2009. But once it was published, both Jane and Adam began to think it was a bigger story, tried to interest someone in a novel version, decided after a couple of rejections that a novella was a better idea. And by that time, Jane was starting a wonderful new publishing relationship with Tachyon, which—surprise!—had a novella program.

Then the hard work really began!

The original short story had been 13,000 words. The novella needed to be closer to 30–35,000. Conversations between the two of us began. And after the first complete novella draft (25,000 words) was done, we burrowed into the history and horror and the astonishing and bloody success that the revolution had been.

A success if you and your family lived through it, that is. Not all of our main characters do make it to the end, though except for Rasputin and the Romanovs and their bloody deaths, we only hint at the others in the novella. Bornstein (Trotsky) made it through the revolutionary years and about twenty years beyond, though he was first exiled from Russia and then escaped to Mexico, where one of Stalin's lackeys (whom he mistook for a friend) took him out with an ice pick to the head.

Along the way, we learned a lot about haemophilia,

the mad monk, the uxorious but-not-particularly-smart last tsar, his unsung wife who really did do a lot for the poor in Russia, though she'd always been considered a foreign interloper who was called called "German Alix" by the courtiers.

Jane felt bad for the murders of the Romanovs, though she always believed that Rasputin got what he deserved. Adam puts it a bit differently: "I feel bad for the children but am pretty solid on my preferred fate for dictators."

The dragons? Mostly, we made them up!

—Jane and Adam

Timelines

1.

The killing of the mad monk, Rasputin, on December 30, 1916 is the stuff of saints' tales or Grand Guignol plays. But for years, the details of his death were exactly as described in our story. Except for the dragons, of course. But new examination of his bones in 2016 seems to show he was more reasonably executed by a bullet to the back of the head. His death, and the death of his influence, would help precipitate the downfall of the Romanovs—

the tsar's family. Frankly, we prefer to believe the mad monk was killed by dragons.

2.

As for the Romanovs, this is the *actual* timeline leading to their brutal murders.

February 1917: Russian Revolution.

After the revolution, the tsar and family are placed under house arrest.

March 15, 1917: The tsar is forced to abdicate.

August 1917: The tsar and family are taken to the Siberian town of Tobolsk.

April 1918: The Romanovs (as the tsar and family are now called) are moved to the Russian town of Yekaterinburg, in the Urals, to a smaller accommodation where the windows of their rooms are painted shut and Anastasia is even shot at when trying to open a window on one stifling summer day.

July 17, 1918: At night, the Romanov family are led into a cellar and there shot, bayoneted, and battered with the barrels of guns. Death by dragons would have been swifter, cleaner, more merciful, so we gave that to them.

For eight years, the new Soviet leadership told lies about the fate of the tsar and his family, even hinting that they were alive and in exile. The Soviets only acknowledged in 1926 that the entire family had been murdered.

In 1981, Nicholas II and his entire family—wife, daughters, and son—were proclaimed *passion-bearers* by the Russian Orthodox Church. A passion-bearer is a saint killed not *because* of his faith, like a martyr, but one who dies *in* faith at the hand of murderers.

1989: The bodies of Nicky and his family were exhumed and re-interred in St. Petersburg, joining most of his forebears back to Peter the Great within the walls of the Cathedral of Saints Peter and Paul.

2018: A hundred years after their deaths, the Romanovs were declared saints. Murdered for their faith. As *The Guardian* has put it: "Yurovsky, the commissar who planned and implemented the killing, was of Jewish background." So it is possible that there was a whiff of anti-Semitism in the canonization.

3.

The Revolutionaries

Trotsky, Lenin, and Borutsch (later Pavel Axelrod) all worked on the Russian revolutionary paper, *Iskra*, whose motto was "From a spark a fire will flare up." Quite a bit on the nose once dragons are involved, but there you go.

In 1903, at the historic Second Congress of the Russian Social-Democratic Labour Party, all three of the men's philosophies diverged, and Borutsch ended up with the Mensheviks opposing Lenin's Bolsheviks. Trotsky started with the Mensheviks but eventually switched his allegiance to the Bolsheviks. It didn't end well for either of them.

The entire minutes from this historic meeting, which lasted for months and had to be moved from Brussels to London partway through due to police interest, can be found online at https://www.marxists.org/history/international/social-democracy/rsdlp/1903.

Koba graduated from robbery, kidnapping, and protection rackets to become one of the most fearsome dictators in all of history, Joseph Stalin.

There were actually two revolutions in Russia in 1917. The February Revolution overthrew the tsarist government and established a provisional government. Just eight months later, the famed October Revolution put paid to all that and established the Soviet government. We largely ignored the February Revolution for purposes of our story, because, well, it didn't last very long and frankly, they didn't have any dragons.

And finally, a note about those larcenous Chinese eunuchs. Jane thought that was way over the top, but Adam showed her the evidence. Yes, larcenous Chinese eunuchs burned down a building in the Forbidden City to hide the fact of their embezzlements in 1923. Well, it was the customs house, not dragon barns. But nevertheless, it stayed in. History is strange enough—even without dragons.

ABOUT THE AUTHORS

Beloved fantasist **Jane Yolen** has been rightfully called the Hans Christian Andersen of America and the Aesop of the twentieth century. In 2018, she surpassed 365 lifetime publications, including adult, young adult, and children's fiction; graphic novels, nonfiction, fantasy, science fiction, poetry, short-story collections, anthologies, novels, novellas, and books about writing. Yolen is also a teacher of writing and a book reviewer. Her best-known books are *Owl Moon*, the How Do Dinosaurs series, *The Devil's Arithmetic*, *Briar Rose*, *Sister Emily's Lightship and Other Stories*, and *Sister Light, Sister Dark*.

Among Yolen's many awards and honors are the Caldecott and Christopher medals; the Nebula, Mythopoeic, World Fantasy, Golden Kite, and Jewish Book awards; the World Fantasy Association's Lifetime Achievement Award, the Science Fiction/Fantasy Writers of America Grand Master Award, and the Science Fiction Poetry

Grand Master Award. Six colleges and universities have given her honorary doctorates.

Yolen lives in Western Massachusetts and St. Andrews, Scotland.

Adam Stemple (www.adamstemple.com) is the author of eight novels, including *Pay the Piper* (with Jane Yolen), winner of the 2006 Locus Award winner for Best Young Adult Book. Of his debut solo novel, *Singer of Souls*, Anne McCaffrey said, "One of the best first novels I have ever read."

Stemple has co-authored two series of novels with Jane Yolen—the *Rock 'n' Roll Fairy Tale* series, and more recently, *The Seelie Wars*. His short fiction includes a series set in feudal Japan featuring a samurai master and apprentice as a sleuthing duo, which was written for the historical fiction magazine *Paradox*.

In addition to writing, Stemple is a musician, web designer, and professional card player. He lives in Minneapolis, Minnesota.